GOBLINS

ON THE PROWL

Read the fantastical prequel to *Goblins on the Prowl*:

Goblins in the Castle

And don't forget these other Bruce Coville titles:

My Teacher Is an Alien
My Teacher Fried My Brains
My Teacher Glows in the Dark
My Teacher Flunked the Planet

GOBLINS

ON THE PROWL

BRUCE COVILLE

J
FIC
COVILLE
2015

Aladdin

New York London Toronto Sydney New Delhi

ALADDIN
An imprint of Simon & Schuster Children's Publishing Division
1230 Avenue of the Americas, New York, NY 10020
First Aladdin hardcover edition June 2015
Text copyright © 2015 by Bruce Coville
Jacket illustration copyright © 2015 by Eric Deschamps
All rights reserved, including the right of reproduction in
whole or in part in any form.
ALADDIN is a trademark of Simon & Schuster, Inc., and related logo is a
registered trademark of Simon & Schuster, Inc.
For information about special discounts for bulk purchases,
please contact Simon & Schuster Special Sales at 1-866-506-1949
or business@simonandschuster.com.
The Simon & Schuster Speakers Bureau can bring authors to your
live event. For more information or to book an event contact the
Simon & Schuster Speakers Bureau at 1-866-248-3049 or visit our website
at www.simonspeakers.com.
Jacket designed by Jessica Handelman
Interior designed by Hilary Zarycky
The text of this book was set in New Baskerville Std.
Manufactured in the United States of America 0515 FFG
2 4 6 8 10 9 7 5 3 1
Library of Congress Cataloging-in-Publication Data
Coville, Bruce.
Goblins on the prowl / by Bruce Coville. — Aladdin hardcover edition.
p. cm.
Sequel to: Goblins in the castle.
Summary: When an accidental spell brings a mysterious stone toad to life, and
it hops away with her human friend William between its jaws, Fauna must use
her magic and her wits to save him, embarking on a journey through dangerous
lands filled with fearsome giants, talking bears, and packs of rogue goblins.
[1. Adventure and adventurers—Fiction. 2. Goblins—Fiction.
3. Magic—Fiction. 4. Friendship—Fiction.] I. Title.
PZ7.C8344Go 2015
[Fic]—dc23
2014043342
ISBN 978-1-4169-1440-2 (hc)
ISBN 978-1-4814-4128-5 (eBook)

*For the kids at Wetzel Road Elementary,
who so joyfully welcomed Igor's annual visit
during all the years I taught there*

CONTENTS

FROM *THE SCRIBBLES OF STANKLO*

(AN INFORMAL HISTORY OF NILBOG)

The first months after William and Fauna, the children from the upper world, healed King Nidrash of his insanity were a time of peace and happiness for the goblin people. Finally free from our imprisonment in Toad-in-a-Cage Castle, we set about restoring our underground city, which had suffered grievous decline during the years of our absence.

Alas, before the year was out, discontent began to stir in Nilbog, a discontent caused by whispers coming from . . . well, no one knew, then, from where. Young goblins — not children, but those just approaching adulthood — began to act rebellious, then disappear. Some in the city whispered they had been taken to the Pit of Thogmoth. That was ridiculous, of course; the Pit had been sealed more than two hundred years before. But where they had gone, or why, no one could truly say.

Goblins are not easily frightened. Even so, fear crept over Nilbog.

That fear grew worse when Flegmire, the mad gobliness who lived outside the city, came to court with her "goblin harmonium." After her concert, which was strangely lovely (I know, for I was there), she stood before the king. When he asked what she

1

wanted, she crossed her arms, then closed her eyes and bowed her head. Her body began to shake. When she looked up again, her huge eyes had the same wild look I had seen the night she'd warned us of our coming captivity. We had ignored her then, and paid a terrible price for that mistake. But what were we to make of this new warning? I can write down her exact words, for they burned themselves into my brain.

"Something dark has come to Nilbog. Something dark and fierce and needy. Promises have been made, and young goblins have believed them. They are out seeking. If they should find what they are after, then something terrible, something terrible—"

She did not finish. Her eyes rolled back into her head, then she screamed and collapsed to the floor. When she finally woke hours later, she had no memory of what she had been saying.

It was many months before we understood her warning. By then it was almost too late.

—Stanklo the Scribbler

When goblins are good, they are very, very good. But when they are bad, they're stinkers.

—*Stanklo the Scribbler*

CHAPTER ONE

INVITATION

It started the day five goblins searched my cottage.

I was setting a snare to catch a rabbit when I heard them coming, though I didn't know yet they were goblins. I stuffed my twine into my pocket and scrambled up a nearby tree. I wasn't afraid, but a girl living alone in the forest has to be careful. I try not to let people see me until I know who they are and what they are up to.

Soon the goblins came into sight. They were being unusually quiet, for goblins, sneaking along with only an occasional fart to announce their presence.

Since I am officially a "Goblin Friend," I should not have been frightened by seeing them. But I could tell something was not right.

The reason I am a Goblin Friend is that I helped my human friend, William, do the goblins a big favor after he freed them from the spell that had imprisoned them in Toad-in-a-Cage Castle for a hundred and twenty-one years.

The reason I was *frightened* was that when William and I had left Nilbog, the goblins had been planning to stay in their underground home for a long time, to recover from their terrible experience in the human world.

So what were *these* goblins doing "up top"? And why were they looking over their shoulders and hiding behind trees, rather than bounding through the forest as goblins normally would?

I waited until they were a little way ahead of me, then dropped to the ground to follow them.

They numbered five in all, two with tails, three without. The shortest stood only a little higher than my waist but seemed to be the leader. They wore red headbands, which I had not seen goblins do before.

It didn't take long to realize they were heading for my cottage. Were they coming with a message . . . or were they planning mischief?

Goblin mischief, when goblins are not crazy, is not too bad. And they tend to make up for it by also doing housework. I wouldn't have minded having them clean up my cottage some. I'd been fixing it up since I'd found it, but it was still a mess. Not that I was going to stay there much longer. The time was coming when I would have to go somewhere else so people wouldn't find out my secret.

Moving had not bothered me in the past, at least not after the first few times. Now that I had met William, the idea was making me sad. But I couldn't let him know the truth about me.

That would be too dangerous.

When the goblins reached the cottage, I slipped behind a tree to watch.

The leader bounced up to the door and called, "Fauna! Fauna, are you there?"

When he got no answer, he threw open the door and bounded in. The others raced to join him. Once they were all inside, I hurried to the west wall, where I crouched to peer through my own window.

To my surprise, the goblins were not doing either mischief or housekeeping. Instead, they were searching for something. They looked under the bed and in the rafters, opened every cupboard, even tried the stones in the fireplace to see if they could find a loose one. And all the while they kept yelling, "Blackstone! Blackstone! Blackstone!"

I was furious and wanted to shout at them to stop. But though I don't mind fighting, I'm not stupid. Five goblins against one girl makes for bad odds.

Finally the leader shouted, "Urxnagle!" which seemed to be some sort of goblin cuss word. "It's not here!"

"Helagon is not going to be happy," whined a green goblin with eyes the size of my fists. "He really wants that thing."

What thing? I wondered. *And who is Helagon?*

"I wish we hadn't agreed to help him," muttered a third goblin, flapping his pointy ears. "He makes me nervous."

"Too late for that!" snapped the tallest goblin. He looked around uneasily, then added, "We should go before we get caught."

"Not until we put everything back!" cried the leader. "Also, we need to make some mischief!"

Leaping about like squirrels, bouncing off the walls, laughing as they worked, the goblins soon had the cottage twice as neat and tidy as when they had entered.

Then they hid my cups and plates under the bed.

That done, they hurried out the door—three running, two rolling—and disappeared into the forest.

I walked to the edge of the clearing, where I sat on a tree stump and stared at my home. What in the world had the goblins been looking for? And who was this Helagon that made them so nervous?

While I was trying to puzzle this out, I heard someone else approaching. This made me cranky. I don't particularly like company, and twice in one day was at least one time too many.

As the footsteps grew closer, I recognized the sound—the clump of a heavy boot, then the slow drag of the other foot. Just to be sure, I slipped behind a nearby tree, then peered around the trunk.

I was right. It was Igor.

Like William, Igor lives in Toad-in-a-Cage Castle. However, until last year no one knew he was there. That's because he lived in the dungeon and made his way around through the secret passages, something the castle has a lot of.

Igor is about a foot taller than me. He would be even taller, but he stoops because of the hump on his shoulder. He's mostly bald but has a bushy black beard that hangs halfway to his knees. His eyes are dark and deep set. His nose looks like a small potato. He always wears a big fur coat, no matter what the weather.

As usual, he was clutching his bear, which is like a

doll, only shaped like . . . well, like a bear. It's made out of fur. I don't know what kind of fur it is, or where he got it, and I don't want to.

Igor uses his bear to bop things that annoy him. A light bop lets you know he is not happy with you. I've seen a mighty bop send a goblin flying several feet into the air.

Igor has never bopped me. I think he knows better.

"Fauna!" he growled when he got closer. "Where you at? Igor got message!"

The growl didn't mean he was angry. Igor almost always growls.

I waited until he had clumped past me, then stepped from behind the tree. I was tempted to tap him on the back, to see if I could startle him, but I knew you should never, *ever* touch Igor's hump. Instead I shouted, "What's the message?"

He spun around, bear raised to battle position. Then his face softened. "Oh, it you. Good job scaring Igor!"

"Thank you."

"Next time Igor scare you instead!"

"You can try."

He scowled but didn't say anything.

"What's the message?" I asked.

Igor scrunched up his face, a sign that he was thinking. Then his eyes went wide and he shouted, "Igor got invitation!"

"Invitation for what?"

"For party!"

"Party?"

I had heard of parties but had never been to one.

"Baron making party for day William free goblins. He call it . . ." Igor stopped and knocked his fist against his head a couple of times. Then he smiled. "He call it Goblin Freedom Day Party!"

"When is the party?"

"On Goblin Freedom Day!"

You have to be patient when you talk to Igor. I took a breath. "Well, when is that?"

Igor scowled, counted on his fingers, and tried twice more. Then his face lit up. "Tomorrow night! It one year from night William free goblins."

"Well, I'm not doing anything then. I guess I can come."

"Good! William will be happy!"

With that, he turned and started back along the path, bear tucked under his arm.

As I watched him go, I realized I wasn't sure what you were supposed to do at a party. I decided to visit Granny Pinchbottom, hoping maybe she could give me some advice. Also, I wanted to tell her about the goblins who had searched my cottage.

Granny Pinchbottom isn't really my grandmother, of course. I don't think she's anyone's grandmother. It's just what people call her.

I didn't used to visit Granny, because I never felt entirely safe when I was with her. That changed after I helped William connect the Goblin King's head to his body. Granny has treated me differently since then. I've even been inside her cottage a few times.

When I got to Granny's clearing, the cottage was gone. This didn't mean anything bad had happened. When Granny isn't at home, her home isn't there either.

Sometimes Granny will show up if she knows I want to visit. So I found a stump to sit on and turned my back to the clearing. I had never actually seen the cottage return, and I was pretty sure it wouldn't if I watched too closely.

I took out my knife and began to whittle at a stick. I didn't whittle it down to nothing. That would have been a waste. Instead, I made a sharp point at the end. When I was done, I set it aside and started on another.

You never know when a sharp stick will come in handy.

About the time I began to shiver from the cold, I heard a rustling behind me. I glanced over my shoulder.

The cottage was back.

Unless you knew better, you would think it had been sitting there for a hundred years.

Granny's cottage has rough walls and a thatched roof. Though a heavy frost had fallen the night before, the rosebush that grows to the right of her door was in full bloom.

It always is.

I knocked, and Granny called for me to enter.

As usual, a three-log fire blazed in the stone fireplace. Also as usual, the black cauldron that hung over the flames bubbled and steamed. You never know about that cauldron. Some days it holds the best stew in the world. Other days the smell coming from it is so disgusting I can hardly stand to stay in the cottage. Once, I saw something climb out of the cauldron, leap to the wall of the chimney, then scramble up into the darkness.

Granny was in her rocking chair, petting Midnight, her huge black cat. She likes to call this "the stroke of Midnight."

The cat yawned, then leaped from Granny's lap to coil around my legs.

"He likes you," Granny said.

Her voice was cracked and dry because she was being her old-lady self. When she looks this way, her hair is limp and gray, her nose long and hooked, her chin sharp and warty. If she wants, Granny can appear as a beautiful young woman. She rarely does, though. I get the feeling she doesn't think it's worth the effort.

I bent to pet Midnight. "I like him back," I said.

Her lap free of cat, Granny got up to stir the cauldron. It was smelling particularly rank. Over her shoulder she said, "So, what brings you to my door this fine day before Halloween? And take off your coat. It's plenty warm in here."

Unbuttoning my coat, I said, "I came about two things."

"Well, that's twice as complicated as usual. Let's start with one."

"A group of goblins searched my cottage today."

Granny's eyes widened. "What were they after?"

"I have no idea! I don't own much, and I can't think of anything I do have that anyone else would want."

"Did they say anything that might give you a hint?"

"They kept shouting 'Blackstone.' But that's not much of a clue."

"There's a Lord Blackstone a day's ride from here.

Hard to imagine he has goblins working for him, though. Anything else?"

"Yes. One of them said, 'Helagon is not going to be happy.'"

Midnight arched his back and yowled.

Granny spun toward me, her eyes blazing.

With a bang the cauldron split open.

Who is Granny Pinchbottom? This is a question that has long puzzled goblins and humans alike. At this time all that can be said is that it is not safe to make her angry.

—Stanklo the Scribbler

CHAPTER TWO

SOLOMON'S COLLAR

"Drat it, girl! Don't startle me like that!"

"Like what?" I asked, backing away from the bright blue goo that was oozing from the cauldron's side.

"Like mentioning Helagon!"

"How was I supposed to know that would startle you?"

It's not wise to sass Granny, but I thought it was unfair for her to blame this on me.

"Never mind," she muttered, which was as close as she would get to admitting I was right. "Be quiet while I take care of this."

She bent, scooped up a handful of the goo, and began to roll it between her palms, drawing up what remained on the floor like someone making a ball of yarn.

Unlike yarn, the goo mushed together.

I wondered why the stuff didn't burn her hands. It had been bubbling hot when the cauldron broke.

As the ball got larger, Granny calmed down. When I thought it was safe to talk, I said, "What was it going to be?"

"I call it 'Restore Life.' It's a new specipe I'm working on."

"Specipe?"

"Combination of 'spell' and 'recipe.'"

"Could it bring back the dead?"

Granny snorted. "Not likely. Which is just as well. Bringing back the dead is generally a bad idea. No, what I hoped this stuff would do is keep someone who is at the edge of death from crossing over, at least for a while. Of course, that was if I finished working on it. Stars alone know if it will work now. Here, take a piece."

I hesitated. The goo looked nasty.

"Take some!" she ordered. She had rolled up most of it now, and the ball was almost too big for her to hold.

It's a bad idea to turn down a gift from Granny, no matter what it is, so I reached forward and touched the goo-ball. It was surprisingly hot.

"Just grab a chunk," she said impatiently.

I plunged in my hand and pulled out a glob. A strand remained attached to the bigger ball of goo.

"Give it a quick, hard tug."

I did as Granny said, and the glob snapped free.

"Now roll it into a ball."

Soon I had a goo-ball of my own, this one the size of an apple. It was surprisingly smooth, as easy to squeeze and shape as bread dough. It wasn't sticky, but it was smelly . . . though not as bad as when it had been cooking.

"What do I do with it?"

"No telling right now." She set the large ball of goo in her rocking chair. "I'll tell you, Fauna, I haven't been that startled in more years than most people have been alive!"

"But how did I startle you?" I asked, amazed that *anything* could surprise Granny.

"It was that name, Helagon. He's a bad one, really bad. What he has to do with goblins is anyone's guess, but it can't be anything good." She made a *V* with her middle finger and pointer finger and spit through it. "You said you had two things you wanted to ask about. What was the other? I hope it's less disturbing!"

"Igor invited me to a party the Baron is having."

I hesitated, then said, "What do you do at a party?"

"Well, what's the party for?"

"To celebrate the day William freed the goblins."

Granny gave me a nearly toothless smile. "Good reason. The Baron was lucky he took that boy in. Now, I'll tell you what. You can have a rose from the bush out front. We'll clear off the thorns, and you can wear it over your ear. That will take care of dressing up."

"Thank you."

"Also, I want to send a gift for William. You can take it for me."

"All right."

I didn't mention that no one had ever given me a gift, but as if she had read my mind, Granny said, "You deserve a gift too. I'm grateful to both of you for what you did. Come on, follow me."

"Where are we going?"

"Downstairs."

"I didn't know you had a downstairs!"

"Did you really think you knew everything about my home?"

I shook my head, because that was the right answer when Granny asked a question like that.

She slid her rocking chair to the side, then pulled open a door in the floor. The space below was dark.

She muttered a few words and snapped her fingers. At once a warm yellow glow rose from the opening.

Midnight coiling around her feet, Granny started down the stairs.

The cellar under the cottage was lit by torches. Torches are usually smoky but these weren't. Also, they had *not* been burning when Granny had opened that trapdoor. . . . She must have lit them when she snapped her fingers.

That is a trick I would like to learn!

In the flickering light I saw that the walls were lined with shelves. On the shelves was an odd mix of bottles, books, bones, clay jugs, glass balls, empty cages, dried lizard skins, and many things I had no name for.

A pair of worktables stretched almost the length of the room. They were covered with tools. I recognized a few . . . hammers and knives, mostly. Others I had never seen before. Some were curved and sharp, some twisty and pointed. They *all* looked pretty nasty.

Strings of garlic, bags of onions, and bunches of dried herbs dangled from the ceiling, making the room smell pleasantly spicy.

Also dangling from the ceiling were dozens of bats.

"Don't they poop on the floor?" I asked.

"Not if they know what's good for them! Now, let's

see what we can come up with." Granny limped to one of the shelves and began to paw through the items. "Ah!" she said, picking up a ball made of yellow glass. She stared at it for a moment, then muttered, "Too dangerous." She tossed it to the floor.

I expected the glass to shatter. Instead, the ball bounced back to the shelf she had taken it from.

She also rejected a silver star, an odd-looking twig, and an ugly-faced doll. At last she picked up a strip of brown leather. Halfway between the two ends, pressed into the leather, was a metal disc with a strange design stamped into its surface.

"This might do," she muttered. Then she nodded and smiled. "Yes, it will do quite nicely!" She handed it to me. "This is Solomon's Collar. When you wear it around your neck, you can speak to animals."

"That's wonderful!"

"Not necessarily. Most animals are more interested in food and shelter than conversation. Still, there are times when it can be useful to ask directions from a hedgehog, or advice from a bear. Doesn't work with bugs, of course, but every once in a while there's a spider you can talk to. All right, that's for William. Let's see what I can find for you."

She returned to the shelf, where she picked up

and discarded a yellowed bone, a chunk of glittering rock, and a foot-long purple feather that began to move as if being blown in the wind. She finally settled on a small green glass bottle about three inches high. A cork stoppered the neck. I could see that the bottle held some kind of liquid.

"What is it?" I asked as she handed it to me.

"Sleep Walk. Enough for four trips—five, if you use it carefully."

"But what *is* it?" I repeated.

Granny grinned, showing her remaining teeth. "When you take a sip, you fall into a deep sleep. Well, your body does. Your spirit remains wide awake . . . meaning you can slip free of your flesh and wander off to observe things without being seen. Well, *mostly* without being seen. A few people might catch a flicker of movement from the corner of their eyes. A very few might think they've seen a ghost." She smiled. "But that's no worry. Everyone needs a proper scare now and then."

"Sounds scary for the person *using* it!"

"It's perfectly safe!" Granny snapped. "Unless . . ."

"Unless *what?*"

She shrugged. "If something happens to your body while you're out roaming—that is, if it should happen to be killed—then you've got no way back in. Which means you end up as one of the wandering dead. So that's unpleasant. Also, you must return to your body within two hours or you'll be shut out forever. But *mostly* it's perfectly safe."

"Thank you," I said, wondering if I would ever have the nerve to use the stuff.

"Don't mention it. Now it's time for you to pay for my advice and counsel. A bit of wood splitting should be just the thing. My stores are down, and it's going to be a long winter."

We climbed the stairs; then she handed me an ax.

I put on my coat and went outside.

I mostly like Granny, but I have to say her idea of "a bit" is different from most people's. In this case "a bit of wood splitting" meant "from now until it's almost too dark to find your way home." Splitting wood is good for warming you up, though. Before long I had taken my coat off again.

Splitting wood is also good for thinking. And what I was thinking about right then was goblins. Why had those goblins left Nilbog? What had they hoped to find in my cottage? Why had they been wearing red headbands?

21

While I was thinking about this, I noticed a squirrel perched on a nearby branch. I wondered what it would be like to talk to it, the way William would be able to do once he had Solomon's Collar.

I took the collar out of my coat pocket and studied it. *It's not like trying it on would wear it out,* I thought.

Looking around to make sure Granny wasn't watching, I placed the metal circle over my throat. Then I pulled the ends of the leather strap behind my neck. As I tried to figure out how to fasten the collar, I heard a soft click and felt a burst of heat against my throat.

I cried out as I realized the collar had fastened itself!

"Is something wrong?" asked the squirrel.

I jumped in surprise. I had understood the thing!

"Well, are you going to talk to me, or nut?" the squirrel asked. Then he chattered with laughter. "Get it?" he cried, clutching his belly. "Talk or *nut?* Oak and beech, sometimes I kill myself!"

I was beginning to understand what Granny had meant when she'd said being able to talk to animals was a mixed blessing.

The squirrel stopped laughing and looked at me, obviously waiting. I realized it was my turn to talk. The thing was, I didn't like talking all that much, even to humans.

"If you're not going to use that collar, you probably shouldn't have put it on," the squirrel said, sounding cross.

"I just wanted to try it."

He smacked his paw against his forehead. I got the feeling he knew something I didn't.

"Fauna!" called Granny. "It's getting dark. Carry in the last load and we'll call it done."

I knew I shouldn't be wearing William's gift, so I reached behind my neck to remove the collar. To my horror, it wouldn't open!

"Uh-oh," said the squirrel. He covered his eyes with his paws, then moved one paw aside so he could watch anyway.

"Go away!" I whispered. "Scat!"

He turned and scampered across the branches.

"Coward," I muttered.

"I may be a coward," he called over his shoulder, "but at least I'm not stupid!"

That stung, because *I* was feeling plenty stupid right then. Plenty scared, too. Granny had clearly told me the collar was for William. I never should have put it on. I thought the squirrel had the right idea in running away, and I longed to do the same. The problem was, the only thing stupider than putting on the collar to begin with would be trying to run from Granny Pinchbottom.

"Fauna! Did you hear me?"

I turned to face the cottage.

Granny was at the door, outlined by the light from her fireplace.

Granny could be kind.

Granny could be helpful.

Granny could turn you into a toad if you made a mistake.

I had made a mistake. I was pretty sure it was a big one.

Though what happened to us in Toad-in-a-Cage Castle was horrific, the humans who live there now are fairly nice. We are still trying to figure this out.

—Stanklo the Scribbler

CHAPTER THREE

THE MYSTERIOUS BOOK

I have learned over the years that fear can be inspirational. In this case it inspired me to put on my coat, then raise its collar and button it around my neck. This hid that other, magical collar, so Granny would not see I was wearing it.

I gathered the last of the wood and headed for the cottage.

"You've got your coat on," Granny said when I reached the door.

"It's cold."

She looked at me sharply but said only, "It's getting dark. Stack the wood over there, and you can be on your way."

Did she know what I had done? I thought so, but maybe it was just my conscience bothering me. Since I didn't really believe I had a conscience, that seemed unlikely. But if she knew, why didn't she say something?

When I had finished stacking the wood, Granny cut a rose from the bush beside her door. She cupped her fingers beneath the blossom, then gave it a shake. The thorns slid off. This made me feel a bit odd. I have always envied the way roses have thorns. They keep people from getting too close.

Tucking the smooth stem over my ear, Granny said, "This will stay fresh for three days."

The small act of kindness made me feel guiltier than ever.

"Give William my greetings," she said.

I promised to do so, thanked her, and started to leave. When I was a few feet from the cottage, she called me back. She looked troubled. I was afraid she was going to scold me about the collar. Instead, she said, "Be careful walking home, and when you go to the castle tomorrow."

This puzzled me. I'm always careful, and Granny knows it. As if she could see the question on my face, she said, "Because of the goblins! There may be more than one mischief out and about."

"I know. I told you, there were five of them."

Granny smiled. "You saw five goblins, but only one mischief."

"I don't understand."

"'A mischief' is the name for a group of goblins. Like 'a flock of birds' or 'a herd of cows' . . . 'a mischief of goblins.' Anyway, be careful. You have been declared a Goblin Friend, but something strange is going on, and you may not be able to count on *all* goblins being friendly to you right now."

I nodded, not happy with this news.

"All right, now scat. Enjoy the party . . . and your gift!"

A prickle ran over my shoulders. Was Granny telling me she knew what I had done with Solomon's Collar?

As I walked away, I felt a mix of fear, confusion, and unhappiness. This annoyed me, since I do not like to feel more than one thing at a time. Then I realized that being annoyed was another feeling. That brought the total up to four, which was even more annoying.

I needed to think. Normally, walking is good for this, because there is no one to bother me. But now that I was wearing the collar, I could hear the animals talking.

And what they were mostly talking about was me.

"That's her!" I heard one rabbit tell another. "The girl the squirrel told us about!"

"Doesn't look as silly as I expected," the other rabbit said. "Certainly not silly enough to have put on that collar when it wasn't meant for her!"

"Never can tell with humans," replied the first. "Even the sensible ones do foolish things sometimes."

"And even the foolish ones can make rabbit stew!" I shouted.

The rabbits scampered into the brush.

I didn't sleep well that night, partly because I was fretting about the collar, partly because several mice were having a party in my wall and they kept singing naughty songs.

Late the next afternoon I slipped the bottle of Sleep Walk into my coat pocket and tucked the rose behind my ear. I hesitated for a moment, then put the ball of blue goo in my other pocket. Then I headed for Toad-in-a-Cage Castle.

I am always cautious in the forest, but this day I was even more so, watching and listening for any sign of goblins.

What was going on with them? Had something

gone wrong in Nilbog? And what could they have been looking for in my cottage?

I was still trying to work this out when I reached the castle.

Toad-in-a-Cage Castle has four towers, one at each corner. The rest of the castle sits between them, which does make it look a bit like a toad in a cage. However, the real reason for its name is that in the center of its Great Hall is a large cage with iron bars as thick as my thumbs. Inside that cage, mounted on a low pedestal, squats an enormous stone toad. From nose to butt it is almost twice as long as I am tall.

The first time I entered the castle, a chill skittered along my spine when I saw the toad. I couldn't say why it frightened me, but it did. The strange thing is, it also fascinated me.

The castle is surrounded by a moat, but the drawbridge was down tonight . . . which makes sense if you are expecting a guest. Actually, the drawbridge was usually down, since there was no war going on and no attacks were expected.

I am always careful crossing the drawbridge. William told me that when he was about five, the woman who took care of him fell off it and was eaten by something.

I would have thought he made this up, except sometimes when I peered over the edge of the bridge, I could see dark shapes gliding through the murky water below.

Big dark shapes.

With enormous eyes.

As I stepped inside the castle, a woman bellowed, "Welcome, Fauna!"

"Hello, Hulda!" I shouted.

Hulda is the Baron's housekeeper. According to William she bellows because she is nearly deaf and has to shout in order to hear herself. You definitely have to shout back to talk to her.

She is plump and cheerful-looking, a little taller than me, and wears her white hair tied in a bun. The most unusual thing about her is that the tip of the index finger on her right hand is missing. When William was little, she told him that Granny Pinchbottom bit it off, and if he didn't behave, the same thing would happen to him.

When Karl, the young man who takes care of the Baron's library, found out about this, he got mad at Hulda for scaring William. That was fine . . . except then he told William that Granny Pinchbottom wasn't real! He claimed she was just someone the old women in the village had invented to scare children into acting properly!

For someone who is so smart, it's amazing how silly Karl can be. On the other hand, I sometimes wonder if William and I are the only people who have actually met Granny. With her, I guess anything is possible.

As for the Great Hall, it could hold my cottage twenty times over. A huge chandelier hangs from the middle of the ceiling, directly above the cage that holds the stone toad. The chandelier has hundreds of candles, but I have never seen them lit. Instead, there are dozens of candles set on various pieces of furniture.

Along the walls stand suits of armor from the olden days.

The mantel over the fireplace holds the Baron's collection of cannonballs from famous battles. They come in a lot of sizes, some no bigger than my fist, some larger than my head.

Hulda led me to the wide stairway that takes you to the second floor, and we went into the dining room. As you would expect, it holds a large table. I had walked around that table once, counting, and figured two dozen people could sit down to dinner without any crowding.

Most times when I visited the castle, the table was

bare. Now it was loaded with wonderful food, including a golden brown roast goose that smelled so delicious my mouth instantly started to water. I had been uncertain about the party, but now I was glad I had come. I just hoped we wouldn't have to wait too long to eat!

A huge fire roared in the fireplace. Standing near it, taking advantage of the warmth, were William, Karl, and the Baron.

William is a bit taller than me. His hair is the color of butter. He has blue eyes, a somewhat pointy nose, and big ears.

Karl is tall and lean, with thick, shiny hair as dark as night. His nose is a little too big, but his eyes are warm and kind. I have been told that the girls in the village think he is handsome.

The Baron is taller than William but shorter than Karl. He has a fringe of hair, very white, around the back of his head. Making up for the lack of hair on top are his bushy eyebrows and huge mustache. His big eyes are pale blue and a bit watery.

The Baron had been kind to me since we'd returned from Nilbog. He'd even invited me to come live in the castle! I wanted to, very badly. I felt safe when I was there. Even more, something about the castle seemed to speak to my heart. But I knew that moving in would only make things worse when it became necessary for me to leave in a year or two. So I had said no.

William, Karl, and the Baron were bending over a big book.

I went to stand beside William. He looked startled when he saw me. I thought it was because he hadn't been expecting me, until he said, "You're wearing a rose!"

I nodded, wondering why he sounded so surprised. I got my answer when he said, "The roses have been gone for over a month. Where did you get that one?"

"Granny Pinchbottom gave it to me." I said it quietly, to avoid getting into an argument with Karl about whether Granny was real.

William smiled. "Ah, now it makes sense. Did she give you that collar you're wearing too?"

"It came from her," I said. Which was true, as far as it went. To change the subject, I said, more loudly, "What's the book about?"

"We're not sure," Karl muttered. "I found it on my desk this morning. Neither the Baron nor I remember ever seeing it before, and we both know the library very well."

"Maybe it's a present for William," I said.

I had presents for William on my mind, since I had accidentally stolen the one I was supposed to give him.

Karl scowled, but William laughed and said, "I like that idea."

"Yes! It for William!" roared a voice from behind me. Igor had entered the room.

"Igor bringed book from dungeon this morning! Igor bringed it for William."

"And where did *you* get it?" Karl asked as Igor thumped toward us.

Igor stopped. He scratched his head. Finally he said, "Lady give it to Igor and say Igor should give it to William."

"What lady, Igor?" asked the Baron.

Before we'd come back from Nilbog, the Baron hadn't even known that Igor was living in the dungeon. He still didn't seem to know what to make of him. This was partly because Igor insists he worked for the Baron's grandfather. Given how old the current Baron is, that would mean Igor has been around for well over a hundred and fifty years.

Igor claims it's a lot longer than that.

"*Who* gave it to you?" repeated the Baron.

Igor smiled, ducked his head, and said, "Pretty lady."

"What was her name?" Karl asked.

"Igor don't remember."

Karl turned to the Baron. "I don't think we should leave this with William. A book like this might be dangerous."

"Any good book can be dangerous," the Baron said. "That should be the definition of a good book."

"Even so, I don't think we should leave it with William."

"It William's book!" roared Igor. "It present from . . . from . . . from Igor!"

"You didn't give it to him," Karl said.

"Bringed it!" Igor growled. "Same thing, almost."

William stepped between them. "Let's say it's my book, but we can keep it in the library. Will that make you feel better, Karl?"

The librarian thought for a moment, then nodded. "Yes. Thank you."

William turned to Igor. "Is that all right with you?"

Igor wrinkled his face, then grumbled, "Guess so."

I could tell by the way he clutched his bear that it wasn't.

"Let's eat!" Hulda shouted. "I spent all day cooking. The food will get cold if we wait any longer."

"Where's Herky?" I asked.

Herky is a little goblin William and I met on our trip to Nilbog. He grew so attached to William that he decided to come "topside" with us and live in the castle instead of staying in Nilbog.

William thinks Herky is cute.

I think he's a pain.

In answer to my question, William shrugged. "Probably off making mischief. He'll show up. He always does."

The goose was as greasy and savory as it looked. Along with it we had potatoes, stuffing, gravy, cabbage, and enough butter to float a small boat.

To top it all off, Hulda brought in a huge cake, five layers high and decorated with fruit and green sugar-goblins. She was about to cut the cake when the Baron coughed. I wondered if he was catching a cold, but when I saw everyone turn toward him, I understood that it was his way of getting our attention.

He raised his glass and said, "I would like to propose a toast."

I scowled. After such a good meal, why would I want toast?

I realized he meant something else when he said, "Here's to William, who set right an old wrong. I had no idea, my boy, that night I found you on the draw-bridge as a baby, how much good you would do in this castle. Bringing you inside was one of the smartest things I've ever done."

He lifted his glass higher. The others raised their glasses too.

So did I, once I realized that this was what people do when they're making "a toast."

"William good!" Igor roared.

Everyone took a drink.

William's face was red. I was starting to think maybe it wasn't such a bad thing that I had never been to a party. *I* wouldn't want that much attention!

But the toasting wasn't over. Raising his glass again, the Baron said, "And here's to Igor and Fauna, also part of the great adventure!"

"To Igor and Fauna!" the others cried.

I wanted to run and hide.

To my relief Hulda bellowed, "Now for the cake!"

She lifted a big knife and sliced into it.

The cake shrieked in pain.

One should always be careful what one puts around one's neck. You would think that people would know this.

—Stanklo the Scribbler

CHAPTER FOUR
TRUTH OR CONSEQUENCES

Hulda screamed, dropped the knife, and staggered back.

At the same moment a little goblin leaped out of the cake, flung himself into William's arms, and cried, "Happy Goblin Freedom Day, butterhead boy!"

It was Herky, of course.

He stands only a bit above my knee but makes enough trouble for someone four times that size. He has big yellow eyes, a nose almost the size of my fist, and pointy ears that flap when he runs. He wore nothing but ragged little britches with a hole in the rear for his tail to stick through. Hulda made better clothing for him, but he refused to wear it.

"What were you doing in that cake?" bellowed Hulda.

Her eyes were blazing. It was a good thing she had dropped the knife when Herky popped out of the cake. If she hadn't, I think she might have decided to use it on him now.

Herky glared at her and cried, "Hulda gave Herky an owieee right on his tail!"

"Herky!" said William sternly. "Answer Hulda. What were you doing in the cake?"

"Being a surprise!" The little goblin's face fell. "Herky bad?"

"Look at the mess you made!" William scolded.

"But look what a good surprise!" Herky replied joyfully.

Life with Herky was like this. In some ways it was excellent to have him around. Goblins like to keep things neat, and William had told me that with Herky living there, Toad-in-a-Cage Castle had been kept spotlessly clean for the first time he could remember.

The thing is, goblins love mischief even more than they love cleaning. Herky never actually *tried* to be naughty. It just came naturally to him. Now he buried his face against William's shoulder and wailed, "Herky been bad! Bad, bad little Herky waited until cake got cool. Bad, bad little Herky made hiding place inside. Herky was soooo careful to be secret. But Herky did bad."

He began to sob. This affected William more than it did me.

Igor watched all this with dismay. I could see he wanted to bop something but couldn't figure out what. The Baron went to the far end of the table and poured another glass of whatever he was drinking. Karl was trying to comfort Hulda, who was moaning about her cake.

I walked to the table. The cake had been way too big for six people and a little goblin. I took out my knife and in a few minutes had seven good-size pieces that hadn't been anywhere near goblin butt.

"Let's have cake!" I said when I was done.

Everyone looked at me in surprise.

"Fauna good!" cried Herky, leaping from William's arms. He knew better than to jump to me, so he landed on the table, where he turned three somersaults, just missing the cake with his feet.

The Baron came back from the far end of the table. "Well done, young lady," he said.

When we finished eating, the Baron gave William and me pocket watches. Personally, I didn't have much use for a watch. It seemed to make William happy, though. The watches were made of gold, with our names and fancy designs engraved on their lids. William's had a sword with vines wrapped around it. Mine had flowers.

I would have rather had the sword.

Even so, I thanked the Baron politely.

I knew the time had come to give William his present from Granny Pinchbottom. Feeling sick, I put my hand to the back of my neck, hoping Solomon's Collar would come off now that I was in front of the person who was supposed to get it.

It didn't.

Fortunately, I had a backup plan. Taking a deep breath, I said, "When I told Granny Pinchbottom about the party, she said she also wanted to send you a gift."

Karl snorted but managed not to say anything.

I held out the bottle of Sleep Walk. "Here it is."

As I spoke the lie, Solomon's Collar tingled.

Then it began to tighten around my neck!

I gasped in panic. Would the collar keep getting smaller until it cut my head off? The fact that when we were in Nilbog I had seen the goblin king's headless body made this all too easy to imagine.

41

"Fauna, are you all right?" William asked. "You look kind of funny."

"I'm fine!" I choked out. This was another lie, and the moment I spoke it, the collar grew even tighter.

"Actually, I'm not. I think I need to sit down!"

Instantly the collar loosened its grip.

Karl rushed over with a chair, and I dropped into it. Sitting there, trying to catch my breath, I realized I had put something around my neck—something I couldn't remove—that would start to strangle me anytime I told a lie.

This did not make me happy.

I know there are worse things that can happen to a person than not being able to lie, but at the moment I couldn't think of any. Lying had been a useful survival tool for me . . . and if you've never been trapped in a room with several angry men, each three times as big as you are, then don't even think of trying to judge me on this.

"It's a good thing you're staying the night," Hulda shouted. "I wouldn't want to send you home not feeling well."

"Staying the night?" I asked in surprise.

Hulda looked equally surprised. "Did you think we'd make you walk home in the dark?"

To be honest—which was the safest thing at the moment—I hadn't thought about it at all. Darkness doesn't bother me that much. That's what torches are for.

Hulda turned to Igor. "Did you forget to tell this poor girl she was supposed to spend the night?"

Igor looked down. "Can't remember," he mumbled.

It was the softest voice I had ever heard him use, so of course Hulda couldn't hear him. "What did you say?" she bellowed.

"Can't remember!" Igor roared back.

Herky scurried under the table. As for me, I was happy to have everyone's attention elsewhere. That didn't last long. Turning back to me, Hulda said, "I meant for you to bring a nightdress. But don't worry. I'll find something you can use."

After that, things settled down. We gathered around the fireplace, and Karl told a wonderfully scary ghost story. When he was done, the Baron got to talking about the old days. This was more interesting than I would have expected, since it turned out he had had a big sister who had vanished when he was a baby.

"Never did find out what happened to her," he said, shaking his head. "Didn't really know her myself. I was too young at the time. My parents never got over

43

it, though." He sighed. "Poor Gertrude. That was her name, Gertrude. I've always wondered what happened to her. Made things hard on me, growing up. My parents were so worried about losing another child, they never let me out of their sight."

He shook his head again. "Listen to me going on! Must be the brandy. Well, that's enough for one night. We should do this again next year, William. And Fauna, of course. Always welcome here, you know, my dear."

That pinched my heart, as I knew that after a year, two at the most, it would no longer be true.

"Come along, Fauna," bellowed Hulda. "I'll show you to your room." She picked up a candlestick that held a thick candle. By its flickering light she led me to the next level of the castle. About halfway down the long hall, she opened a door and shouted, "Here you go!"

The room was bigger than my entire cottage. A lovely fire blazed in the fireplace. The bed, high as my waist, was wide enough for four people. Against the opposite wall stood a tall wooden box with two doors. Carved into the doors were beautiful images of dragons and unicorns.

Hulda used her candle to light the one on the

nightstand next to the bed. "Wait here," she said, then scurried out of the room. While she was gone, I pulled open the doors of the tall wooden box.

It was empty.

As I closed the doors, Hulda returned with a white shirt. "This used to belong to the Baron," she said. "You can use it to sleep in."

After she left, I took the rose from behind my ear and placed it on the table beside the bed. Then I slid out of my clothes and put on the shirt. It was amazingly soft.

I climbed into the bed and blew out the candle. The fire, low but still burning, cast a dim light into the room.

I tossed and turned but couldn't get comfortable. The bed was soft. Too soft. I was about to climb out and sleep on the floor when I heard a creak from the tall wooden box.

I sat up and swallowed hard. The door of the box swung open. As I reached for my knife, a cheerful voice called, "Hey, Fauna. You still awake?"

"William? What are you doing here?"

"I wanted to ask you about this bottle you gave me."

He stepped out of the box. He held a candlestick in one hand, and by its flickering light I saw that he was fully dressed. Also, he had a rat on his shoulder.

The rat's name is Mervyn. William had trained the little beast to eat out of his hand.

He is fonder of rats than I am.

Mervyn lifted his head, stared at me for a moment, then said, "What in the name of the High Holy Rat is that thing around your neck?"

Actually, he made a series of squeaks.

Even so, I understood him perfectly.

William turned his head to glance at Mervyn, clearly startled by the rat's sudden outburst.

"It's called Solomon's Collar," I said.

William looked at me oddly. "Fauna, are you talking to Mervyn?"

My face got hot, and I nodded.

"Since when do you talk to rats?"

"Good question," Mervyn chittered.

I was ashamed to tell William I had accidentally stolen his gift. On the other hand, if I didn't want to get choked, whatever I told him had to be true. Thinking carefully, I put my hand to my neck and said, "It's this collar. It lets me talk to animals."

Not the entire story, but true as far as it went.

William's eyes lit up. "Wow! I wish I had something like that."

I was glad the light was too low for him to see me blush.

"Anyway, I came to ask about this." He held up the little green bottle. "Right after you handed it to me, you had that almost-fainting spell. Then things got going and . . . well, you never did tell me what it's for. Should I drink it?"

"No! At least, not yet. Let me explain how to use it."

When I was done telling him about Sleep Walk, and what he had to be careful of, he lifted the bottle and said, "Sounds useful but scary."

"It sounds insane!" Mervyn squeaked.

Deciding not to translate *that*, I said, "'Useful but scary' probably describes most things that come from Granny Pinchbottom."

I was confident the collar would not squeeze my neck for *that* sentence.

William slipped the bottle into his pocket and said, "Let's go look at my other present." When I looked puzzled, he added, "You know, that book Igor brought from the dungeon."

"I thought Karl wanted you to stay away from it."

"I told Karl I would leave it in the library. I didn't say I wouldn't look at it!"

I smiled, which William understood to mean I was with him.

"Better get dressed," he said. "The castle is cold at night."

"Well, I'm not getting dressed in front of you. Go out into the hall!"

Once I had on my regular clothes, I opened the door. I expected to step out and follow William to the library. Instead he walked in and crossed to that big wooden box.

"What is that thing, anyway?" I asked as he opened the door.

"It's called a wardrobe. It's used to hold clothes."

"Or dead bodies," Mervyn added.

I was fairly sure the rat was joking. I was not amused. The last thing I needed was a talking rat who thought he had a sense of humor.

"If it's for clothes, why are you opening it now? And how did you get into it to begin with? I checked before I went to bed, and it was empty."

"I wasn't in it then, silly. This isn't *just* a wardrobe. It's also an entry to the secret passages. Better for getting around the castle at night if we don't want people to know what we're up to."

"Ah," I said, moving closer.

William ran his hands over the back wall of the wardrobe. Something clicked, and with a hiss the wall moved to the side. Beyond was nothing but darkness.

"Hand me the candle," William said. "You should grab one too."

I fetched my candle from the nightstand, lit it from William's, then followed him into the narrow passageway. After a while we came to a stairway. We followed it down to the next floor.

At the bottom of the stairs William began to count as we walked.

"What are you—"

"Shhh!"

When he reached forty, he stopped and whispered, "This should be the spot. Bring your candle closer. I need more light."

I did as he asked. A second later he said, "See?"

The only thing I saw was a bat clinging to the wall.

William reached for it.

"Don't!" I cried.

He chuckled, grabbed the bat, and slid it to the side.

A section of wall went with it.

"The bat is carved from wood," Mervyn explained.

"It's like a doorknob but more interesting," William

added, though he couldn't have known what Mervyn said.

We stepped into the library. William had told me that the Baron had knocked out the walls between seven rooms to make enough room for all his books. Our candles lit only a small area in that enormous space.

"Where do you suppose *your* book is?" I whispered.

"Karl's desk, probably. Come on. It's that way."

"I'm not sure this is a good idea," muttered Mervyn.

"What did he say?" William asked. When I translated, William said, "Tell him he doesn't need to stay if he doesn't want to."

I told the rat what William had said.

Mervyn laughed. "I'm not the one I'm worried about! It's William who tends to get into trouble. He has a gift for it."

"He says he'll stay," I told William. I left out the rest, not wanting to get caught in an argument between a boy and his rat.

William nodded and continued into the library. When we reached Karl's desk, we lit more candles. They created a small circle of brightness in the vast gloom.

The surface of Karl's desk was empty, the book nowhere in sight.

William said a bad word, then tried to open the drawers.

They were locked.

He said an even worse word.

"Let me try," I said.

William stepped aside. I unstrapped my knife and inserted the tip into the space between the top of one drawer and the desk itself. I slid it along until it hit something. I began to tap at the blockage, and a moment later it released. I slid the drawer open.

William gaped at me. "Who taught you to do that?"

"A person I used to know," I said, not wanting to get into details. That had been a particularly bad year.

William's book wasn't in the drawer, so I tried the matching one on the other side.

"Aha!" cried William. "Got it!"

I hadn't had a chance to get a good look at the book before. In the flickering light of our candles, I saw that the black leather cover had strange designs stamped in the surface. Something about them made me shudder.

William seemed to sense the strangeness too. "This thing is weird," he whispered.

As he spoke, the book opened.

By itself.

I looked down at the page and gasped.

William—whom the goblins refer to as "the William," for the wonderful service he did us—is a great hero in Nilbog. Even so, we do recognize that he sometimes acts a bit unwisely.

—Stanklo the Scribbler

CHAPTER FIVE

BUFO ANIMA!

"That's the stone toad in the Great Hall!" I said, pointing to the picture in the book.

"Definitely," William replied.

I motioned to the facing page. "Those letters are weird. Can you figure them out?"

He stared at the words for a long time. Finally he said, "The writing is really old-fashioned, but I think I can read it." Holding the candle above the book, he said, very slowly, "'This is the Toad of Stone, which is said to hold a secret both dangerous and powerful. According to *The Book of Dark Charms*, the spell will one day be broken by a youth with much to learn.'"

I shivered. "What spell? And what do you suppose will happen when it's broken?"

"Don't have any idea. There's more. A kind of, oh, prophecy, I guess. Listen:

"Evil does not sleep eternal
And Black Stone will not stay concealed.
Power dark and strength infernal
At wizard's hand will be revealed.

In Nilbog's depths the final act,
It's there that all is lost or won.
Will goblin world remain intact,
Or darkness grow when battle's done?

Homeless spirit, ageless roamer,
Two hungry souls must play their roles.
One needs body, one must know more,
But what the price of such dear goals?

The fate of all rests in their hands,
The cost so high it stills the voice.
Long-buried hope makes sharp demands;
A breathless world awaits their choice. "

When he was done, I said, "What in the world is *that* supposed to mean?"

"Who knows? It's the first I've heard anything about the toad having a spell on it, much less a connected prophecy." He paused, looked at me strangely, then whispered, "Do you feel that?"

I knew what he meant . . . a sudden chill in the air. "Must be a window open," I said.

I was wrong. We learned the real reason for the chill when William said, "I want to know who asked Igor to bring me this book to begin with."

Suddenly Solomon's Collar began to tingle. At the same moment a voice from behind us said, "I think I can answer that."

We spun around, and I let out a little squeak.

I think the squeak was justified, since I could see right through the man who was standing there. Other than that, and the fact that the side of his head had been bashed in, he appeared fairly normal. He had large eyes, a big nose, and a down-turned mouth. He looked older than Karl but younger than the Baron. He also looked as if he spent most of his time feeling sad, which made sense for someone who had had his head bashed in.

"Sorry you can't see me," said the man, obviously

54

not realizing that I could. His voice was high, and he spoke in a snooty way. "It's one of the side effects of being dead."

"So you're a ghost?" William asked.

I could tell from William's face that he really couldn't see the ghost. However, from the way Mervyn was staring, I got the feeling the rat *could* see him.

I was pretty sure the reason *I* could see the ghost was Solomon's Collar. That tingle must have been a sign that the thing was working. I wondered how many other powers the collar might have.

I decided not to tell the ghost I could see him. It can be very useful to be able to do something people don't know about.

The ghost floated close to William. "Yes, genius boy, I'm of the spirit world. You didn't imagine this castle *wasn't* haunted, did you? I really am sorry you can't see me, because you're missing the way I'm rolling my eyes right now."

I *could* see it, of course, and it made me want to smack him.

"I've lived here for eleven years," William said. "How come I never knew about you before?"

"I never had anything to say to you before. It's not like I go around trying to be noticed. Life—or, in my case, death—is simpler if you don't attract too much attention."

"How long ago did you die?" I asked.

"Not sure. It's tricky to keep track of time once you leave your body. Don't need to eat, don't need to sleep, so the things that normally mark off the days are gone."

"Why are you still here?" William asked. "From what I understand, most people move on after death."

"And a good thing they do! Can you imagine how crowded it would get if everyone who had ever lived stayed hanging around in spirit form? You couldn't walk across a room without passing through half a dozen ghosties!"

That thought made me shiver.

"Very interesting," said William. "Even so, it doesn't answer my question. Why are *you* here? Were you murdered horribly and need revenge? Are your bones undiscovered and waiting to be buried? Did you commit some terrible crime you have to make right before you can move on?"

"Curiosity killed the cat," the ghost said, and sniffed. "And it's not going to do you any good either. You haven't done anything to earn hearing my life story, much less my death story."

He was getting cranky. Fearing he might leave with the most important question unanswered, I blurted, "You said you could tell us who asked Igor to bring William this book."

"Ah! A point to the young lady for remembering what this is really about! As a reward I shall tell you my name. It's Werdolphus."

Trying not to laugh, I said, "Thank you. I feel honored. Now can you tell us who gave the book to Igor?"

"Yes. Her name is Sophronia. She visits the Baron once a year. When she does, she stops in the Great Hall, grasps the bars of the cage, stares at the toad, and weeps silent tears. It's very sad."

"How did she get into the dungeons?" William asked.

"Don't know."

"Is she good or bad?" I asked.

"Don't know."

I considered making my next question "What good are you?" but decided it would not be useful. So I held my tongue and let William continue the conversation.

"Why did this Sophronia want Igor to give the book to me?" he asked.

Werdolphus sighed. "Look, you understand I can't leave the castle, right?"

This surprised me into speaking. "Why not?"

The ghost spread his arms. "Those of us who have not 'moved on,' as people so quaintly call it, tend to be place-bound. Usually it has to do with how we died—*which I am not about to tell you!* Anyway, the point is, being held here, I don't know a lot about Sophronia or what she's up to. It's not as if I can follow her when she leaves! All I know is that she visits once a year and always takes time to inspect the stone toad when she does."

"That's interesting in itself," William said. "The Baron doesn't have many visitors."

"Yes, and the ones he does have are pretty strange. This one, for instance, has been visiting the Baron since well before I died, and she doesn't look a day older than the first time I saw her. So I would be careful if I were you. I have no idea why she wanted Igor to bring you that book, but I doubt it was simply to enrich your education. Of course, back when I was alive, my friends often accused me of being overly cautious. A ridiculous charge, especially given how I died."

Before I could stop myself, I asked, "How *did* you die?"

A look of fury twisted the ghost's face. "I told you I wasn't going to answer that!" he cried.

Then he vanished.

"He's gone," William said.

I knew Werdolphus was gone, of course, since I had seen him go. But I wondered how William had figured it out. "How do you know?" I asked.

"It's not so cold anymore."

I realized he was right. "Sorry I asked him that question," I said. "I didn't mean to drive him away."

William shrugged. "He was pretty touchy. One of us would have offended him sooner or later. It's too bad, though. I wonder how much more he could have told us. The big thing we've learned is that we have to be careful with this book."

"It's a book. Ink on a page. How dangerous can it be?"

"The Baron claims books can be screamingly dangerous. He says the only thing more dangerous than reading them is trying to hide what's in them."

This didn't make much sense to me, but I decided not to press the point. Instead, I asked, "What are you going to do about this one?"

"We need to study it."

This sounded boring, since it would mean William sitting and reading his book while I stood and watched. Or sat and watched. Boring either way. Suddenly I had an idea. "Let's take it downstairs!"

"Why?"

"Reading about the toad is fine. But the real thing is right there in the Great Hall. Wouldn't it make sense to study the toad at the same time you're studying the book?"

"Brilliant!"

I decided not to explain that I'd made the suggestion just to keep from getting bored.

We put out the candles except for the ones we would carry. William tucked the book under his arm, then led the way back to the secret passage. We went down to the next level and entered the Great Hall through a sliding panel behind a suit of armor.

The first thing we did was light more candles— the place was well stocked with them—and arrange some in a circle around the cage. The candles created a small pool of light in the center of the Great Hall. Beyond that, all remained dark and shadowy.

William slipped between the bars and climbed onto the toad's back. "Did I ever tell you this is one of my favorite places for thinking?"

"Did I ever tell you that you are a very strange boy?"

He rolled his eyes. "Hand me a candle."

I did as he asked. He put the candleholder on the toad's head, positioning it between two stone warts that were as big as his fists. Then he opened the book.

Mervyn scrambled off William's shoulder, down the toad's rump, and over to my feet. "Pick me up," he squeaked.

"Why?"

"He ignores me when he's reading."

"Poor rat," I said as I lifted him to my shoulder.

"Sarcasm is not welcome," he replied, tugging a strand of my hair.

As William studied the book, I slipped into the cage and began to study the toad, examining it from all sides. As always, something about it disturbed me. When I got to the toad's rump, William called, "Fauna, how many candles did we put around the cage?"

I did a quick count. "Five. Why?"

"Well, that's convenient. It says here, 'If you would learn what's hid beneath the toad, then candles five around him star-shape place.'"

"How can anything be hidden beneath the toad? It's sitting on a chunk of solid stone!"

Instead of answering me, William continued to read: "'Three times widdershins walk about the cage. As lines that shine . . .' Drat! Someone has blotted out the next words!"

It turned out the missing words didn't matter. I

had been walking around the toad as I studied it, and on the third circle I noticed something I had never seen before: At the back of the low pedestal on which the toad squatted were four thin lines. They formed a rectangle about five inches high and two feet wide.

I knelt and traced the lines with my fingertip.

They grew warm and began to glow a soft yellow.

"Well, *that's* interesting," Mervyn said.

I ran my finger over the lines again, and they glowed more brightly.

I heard William reading aloud from the book once more.

I ran the tip of my finger around the rectangle a third time, and a drawer slid out of the pedestal. It held a round mirror the size of a large platter. Attached to it was a leather cord, as thick as my little finger.

I lifted the mirror to examine it.

William continued to read from the book.

I gazed into the mirror, then cried out and nearly dropped it. My face had disappeared. In its place was a gnarled and twisted man who wore a robe and a pointed hat. As I watched, he was struck by a blast of blue light. He made a face as if crying out. Then— more quickly than I can write these words—he became a toad!

A stone toad.

A very large stone toad.

After a moment the man reappeared, and the scene repeated itself. I began to tremble. Something about the scene was weirdly familiar. *Why?*

"Um, William . . ."

He continued to read out loud. I looked at him and realized he wasn't reading after all—how could he be? His eyes were closed!

"William!" I cried.

At the same time he shouted, *"Bufo anima!"*

Which was when the stone toad started to move.

Messing about with magic almost always leads to trouble. Oddly, this doesn't seem to keep people from doing it.

—Stanklo the Scribbler

CHAPTER SIX

TONGUE-TIED

At first the toad's movement was slow—so slow, I wasn't sure if it was real or a trick of the candlelight. Then I saw it again, a flex of the hind leg.

"Oh, jeez," said Mervyn. "That can't be good!"

"William, get down," I called. "Get down!"

At the same time, I backed up. When I bumped into the iron bars, I turned and slipped out of the cage.

"William! The toad is moving!"

He continued to chant.

I threw a candle at him, trying to get his attention. I missed, and he kept on chanting. I flung the mirror to the floor, hoping a loud noise would bring William out of his trance. It worked. He started, as if roused from sleep, then cried, "What's going on?"

"The toad is coming to life! Get down, get down!"

The toad flexed its shoulders.

With a cry of horror William slid to the floor, then squeezed through the bars. "What have we done?" he whispered.

"I don't know. But whatever it was, we didn't do it alone. Something put you into a trance."

"What?"

"I'll explain later!"

"Should we run?"

I shook my head. "As long as the toad is still in the cage, we should be all right. We'd better stay and see what happens."

We watched the toad. It hunched its shoulders.

Its nostrils twitched.

Then it opened its eyes.

Though its body remained stone gray, the eyes—bigger than apples—were gold with flecks of brown. The creature blinked twice, then stretched its right front leg forward. The candle William had placed on its head clattered to the stone floor.

The toad's body began to shake, almost as if it was going to throw up. I heard a loud clunk but couldn't see what caused it. And I wasn't about to go look, because next the toad used its front legs to grasp a pair of the iron bars. It pulled on them, clearly straining.

With a horrible creaking sound the bars bent to the toad's strength.

William and I backed away. As we did, the toad leaned sideways and began to pull itself through the opening.

Moving as one, William and I ducked into the shadows beyond the circle of the candlelight. I wanted to run but couldn't tear my eyes from what was happening. But when the toad turned and leaped in our direction, we did run.

We moved too late. I heard a *thwap!* and a *whoosh*, followed by a horrified cry. When I turned to look, I saw that the toad had nabbed William as if he was a giant fly! My friend was now clamped in the toad's mouth, head sticking out on one side, feet on the other. He bellowed and squirmed, but the toad's grip never loosened.

I stood, frozen in horror, terrified that the monster was about to swallow William. Fortunately, William was too big for that. Or maybe it was just that the toad had him sideways and couldn't get him down.

"Fauna!" William cried. "Fauna, help!"

Coming to my senses, I pulled out my knife and

started toward the toad. I was scared, but that was my friend in the monster's mouth!

The creature turned and with a single hop made it halfway to the door that led to the drawbridge. The thud of its landing shook the floor.

I rushed forward, shouting, "Let him go, you monster!"

The toad turned to look at me. The gaze of those golden eyes stopped me in my tracks. Then I remembered that I was wearing Solomon's Collar. Had the creature understood me?

Holding my knife in front of me, I growled, "Put my friend down."

I hoped the toad would talk back and accidentally release William. Instead, it narrowed its eyes and stared at me.

Until that moment I hadn't known a toad could look surprised.

"Let me go!" howled William, shaking his head from side to side. *"Let me go!"*

Behind me someone shouted, "Hey, that *my* William!"

Turning, I saw Herky standing on the banister. Flinging himself into the air, he cried, "Let go of my William, you booger!"

The little goblin landed on the toad's butt, scampered up its spine, and began to jump up and down on its head.

Herky's arrival jolted me into action. Waving my knife, I started forward again. As I did, the toad took another mighty leap and struck the door full force. The door buckled, and the toad sailed through. Herky almost slipped off but by grabbing one of the toad's warts managed to hold on.

I wondered if the creature was made of some kind of living stone. It had to be tougher than the average toad or it would have broken its nose bashing through the door that way.

The drawbridge was still down, which was good. If it had been raised, the monster might have bashed through that, too, and landed in the moat. Even if it had sunk straight to the bottom, it probably would have made it to the other side, since anything that had tried to bite it would have lost some teeth. But one of those huge things I'd seen swimming there would probably have chomped off William's head and feet before the toad climbed up on the far bank.

"Stop, you bad toad!" shrieked Herky, who still clung to the toad's skull. "Stop, stop!"

I raced after them, but the toad was too fast. Each

leap carried it ahead by another ten or fifteen feet, almost as if it were flying. Every time it landed, the bridge shuddered and boards splintered and broke.

Clearing the bridge in four mighty hops, the toad vanished into the darkness.

The last things I heard were Herky shouting "Stop, you bad toad!" and William's desperate cry of "Fauna! Get Igor!"

I wanted to go after them but couldn't follow the trail in the dark without a torch. And I knew I couldn't defeat the toad on my own. So I did as William asked and headed back to get Igor.

When I entered the Great Hall, I found Karl standing in front of the cage. He was dressed in a nightshirt and holding the book. "What in the world have you done?" he cried, shaking the book at me. "I tried to tell everyone this was dangerous! What happened to the toad?" He looked around. "And where is William?"

Before I could answer, Igor thundered into the room. Unlike Karl, he was dressed in daytime clothes—his usual fur coat and boots. "What happen?" he bellowed. "Where William?" He looked at the cage, then added, *"Where toad?"*

I started to answer, but before I could get three words out, a voice from above called, "What in the name of Hercules' bright pink underwear is going on down there?"

It was the Baron. Like Karl, he was dressed in a nightshirt. Holding a candle before him, he tottered down the stairs.

"The toad came to life!" I shouted before anyone could interrupt me. "It wrapped its tongue around William and hopped away with him! We have to go after them!"

"Good heavens!" cried the Baron. "How in the world did that happen?"

I wanted to answer, but half expected Hulda to show up in the next few seconds. Then I realized that, unlike the others, she would not have heard the commotion. So I started to talk.

The Baron, Karl, and Igor listened, wide-eyed, as I told the details of the last few minutes. I would have preferred to hide my part in it, but with Solomon's Collar ready to choke me if I told a lie, it was safer—and faster—to tell the truth.

"Hard to tell whether it was what William was reading or what Fauna was doing that brought the creature to life," Karl said when I finished.

"Likely some combination of the two," replied the Baron.

"Blame us later!" I cried. "Right now let's go get William!"

The Baron turned his great, watery eyes on me. "My dear Fauna, there is nothing I desire more than to rescue young William. But we have to know what we're dealing with! No point in rushing into the darkness with no idea what we're facing."

"But the toad might eat him!"

Karl shook his head. "If it had wanted to eat William, it could have done so right here. You're tough, Fauna, but I doubt you could have stopped him. It. Whatever. The thing could have shot its tongue out again and used William to knock you over. Instead, it wanted to get out of here." He wrinkled his brow. "And for some reason it took William with it. The question is, *why*?"

"That what Igor want to know!" shouted Igor, stomping in a circle and waving his bear over his head.

"Had no idea there was a drawer in that pedestal," the Baron muttered. "Where's that mirror you mentioned, Fauna?"

I found it on the floor and handed it to him. I blushed as I did. It had cracked when I threw it down to bring William out of his trance.

"Almost big enough to be a shield," muttered the

71

Baron. "Plain-looking thing, though. Wonder what this cord was for?"

"What difference does it make?" I cried. "We have to go get William!"

"Yes! Yes! Go get William!" roared Igor.

"The more we know about the toad before we start, the better our chances of succeeding," Karl replied. Turning to the Baron, he said. "What do the castle records say about the toad?"

The Baron tugged at the ends of his mustache and said, "Haven't looked at 'em in ages. The thing was brought here for safekeeping when I was a little boy. Never seemed like you needed to do much to keep it safe, except maybe dust it on occasion. I don't remember any warnings about it being likely to come to life."

Karl sighed. "I'd better dig into the archives. Did you notice the message inscribed on the pedestal?"

"Didn't even look," huffed the Baron, moving to see what Karl meant.

I went with him. Standing beside him, I could see the words that had been hidden until now by the toad's body: BEWARE OF HELAGON.

I shuddered. The goblins who had searched my cottage the day before had talked about Helagon. But the toad had been covering this warning for almost as long as the Baron had been alive. How old was this Helagon person if he had been dangerous even back then?

"I've seen that name in one of the books," said Karl. "If I remember correctly, it was not connected with anything good."

"Wait a minute," said the Baron. He raised his forefinger as if he was about to make an important point. "I remember my father saying something about a man—a wizard, actually—named Helagon. He'd come here asking about—"

The Baron made a gasping sound.

Then his eyes rolled back in his head and he crumpled to the floor.

Goblins find warrior women fascinating but slightly terrifying. We never want to be on their bad side.

—Stanklo the Scribbler

CHAPTER SEVEN

BWOONHIWDA

Karl rushed to the Baron's side.

"Did he faint?" I asked.

Karl shook his head. "I don't think so. I think he was about to tell us something that someone else didn't want us to hear."

I dropped to my knees and patted the old man's cheeks. "Baron! Baron, wake up!"

He moaned but didn't rouse. His skin had gone dead white.

"Igor, fetch some water!" Karl ordered.

"Water!" Igor grunted. "Good idea!" He clumped off in the direction of the kitchen.

I put my ear to the Baron's chest. His breathing was

steady, but his heartbeat seemed weak. Since I didn't know how his heartbeat usually sounded, it was hard to tell what this meant. Even so, it scared me.

Igor returned with a large pitcher. He handed it to Karl, who dipped in his fingers, then flicked a few drops of water onto the Baron's face.

Nothing happened.

Karl scooped out a handful and dribbled it over the Baron's face.

Nothing.

He dumped the entire pitcher over the Baron's head.

The old man didn't even twitch. The only change was that now his hair was slicked back and his mustache was dripping.

"Not good," Igor said, squeezing his bear to his chest.

"Not good, and clearly a magical sleep," Karl replied.

I put my ear back to the Baron's chest.

His heartbeat was weaker than before.

I grabbed Karl's arm. "Listen," I said urgently.

He did, and his face grew almost as pale as the Baron's. "He's dying," he whispered. He covered his face with his hands and began to weep.

I headed for the stairs.

"Where Fauna go?" Igor bellowed.

"Be right back!" I shouted.

I raced up to my room, dug into my coat pocket, and pulled out the blue goo Granny Pinchbottom had given me. Her "specipe"—the one I had interrupted—had been for something to keep someone from dying. She'd said she had no idea if it would work or not, but I couldn't think of anything else to do.

Only, how the heck was I supposed to use the stuff?

I hurtled back down the stairs. Karl still knelt beside the Baron. Igor was clutching his bear so tightly that if it had been alive, he would have strangled it. I dropped down beside the Baron and broke off a chunk of the goo about half the size of my thumb. Not knowing what else to do, I pulled open the Baron's mouth and shoved it in.

"What are you doing?" Karl screamed.

"Quiet! Let's see if this does any good."

I held my breath, growing more fearful as the seconds passed. Then I saw it. . . . Color was returning to the Baron's cheeks! I pressed my ear to his chest a third time, then said to Karl, "Listen!"

He put his own ear to the Baron's chest. "His heartbeat is better!" He looked at me suspiciously. "What did you put into his mouth?"

I held up the goo.

"What is it?"

"It was supposed to be something called Restore Life. I got it from Granny Pinchbottom."

Karl looked like he wanted to argue but didn't know what to say. Before he could say anything at all, a squeaky voice cried, "Herky back! Herky back!"

Looking up, I saw the little goblin bound through the door the toad had smashed open. To my surprise he was followed by a very big woman. She was about Karl's height but probably weighed three times as much. She wore a metal helmet that sported a pair of curved horns. From beneath the helmet flowed two thick blond braids that hung past her knees. Several knives were inserted into the braids, all in sheaths, of course. Woven into the bottom of each braid was a heavy-looking ball.

She took one look at the empty cage and let out a shriek that shattered the glass pitcher Igor had brought water in.

"Sowwy!" she said. "When I get excited, I tend to bweak gwass. My name is Bwoonhiwda, by the way," she added, putting out an enormous hand for Karl to shake.

"Brunhilda?" Karl asked, wincing at the power of her grip.

The woman shot him a glare and said, very clearly, "*Bwoonhiwda* . . . just wike I said!"

"Are we under attack?" cried a familiar voice.

It was Hulda, and the fact that Bwoonhiwda's shriek had woken her was proof of how powerful it had been. Hulda bustled down the stairs now in a white nightdress. Her silvery hair was unpinned, and it flowed past her waist. I had had no idea it was so long.

"Are we under attack?" she repeated. Then she spotted the Baron. With a cry she hurried to his side and got to her knees. "What happened?" she demanded as she stroked his forehead.

After Karl loudly explained, she said, "There's magic at work here, and not good magic either." Looking past him, she noticed the big woman. "And who are *you*?" she demanded.

I turned to study the woman more closely myself. For a top she wore something made of metal. She had a large bosom, and I could not imagine that the armor was comfortable. She wore leather trousers and clutched a spear. A long cloak, bright red, hung from her shoulders.

"Yes, who are you?" asked Karl, repeating Hulda's question.

"And why are you here?" demanded Hulda.

"Herky bringed her!" cried the goblin, dancing about in excitement.

"Herky!" I said sternly. "Where is William?"

His shoulders drooped. "Toad still got William."

"Why didn't you stay with him?"

"Herky tried! But big branch bonk Herky. Branch knock Herky off toad. Herky land on head. Another bonk! Bonks made Herky sleep. When Herky open eyes again, toad gone!" He started to cry. "Herky bad to let toad go! Bad, bad, bad little Herky!"

I sighed. "You're not bad, Herky. You did better than me."

"I found him in the woods, wooking dazed," Bwoonhiwda said.

As she spoke I noticed Igor gazing at her as if she was the most amazing thing he had ever seen.

"What were you doing in the forest to begin with?" Karl asked.

"The queen's wizahd pwedicted a pwobwem with

the stone toad. So the queen sent me to wook into it. Awas, I see I am too wate."

"Why would the queen send a woman to investigate a situation like that?" Karl asked.

Bwoonhiwda shot him such a look, I was surprised his hair didn't burst into flames.

Karl, who sometimes acted as if he knew something about *everything*, blushed. But he didn't give up. "May we have some proof that you really come from the queen?" said Karl.

Bwoonhiwda reached into her cloak and pulled out a scroll that she handed to Karl. He unrolled the parchment. When I stepped next to him, he pointed to a blob of red wax at the bottom. It had the image of a dragon pressed into it. "The royal seal," he told me. "Queen Wilhelmina really did send her."

"Good! Since her job is to look into problems with the stone toad, *let's go look for the thing!*"

"One thing at a time, Fauna!" Turning back to Bwoonhiwda, he said, "How did you end up here at this time of night?"

Bwoonhiwda thumped the butt of her spear against the floor. Standing very straight, she said, "I had made camp and gone to bed, pwanning to come to you at sunwise. As I was dwifting off to sweep, a howwid commotion woke me. When I went to investigate, I found this wittle gobwin. He had been knocked sensewess."

I considered pointing out that Herky was senseless even when awake, but decided to keep that to myself.

"Once I managed to wouse him, he said he had been chasing a giant toad. Then he wed me back to you."

She looked around and shook her head, as if she couldn't understand what she was seeing. I realized what a strange group we made—a small goblin, Igor (whatever he was), Karl and Hulda in their nightshirts, the Baron passed out cold on the floor, and me. *I* certainly didn't look as if I belonged in a castle.

After studying us for a moment, Bwoonhiwda said, "What, exactwy, has happened heah?"

Naturally, that question required yet another explanation of everything that had gone on earlier. When I finished telling my part of it, I turned toward Karl and added loudly, *"And now we need to look for William!"*

"I'm not disagreeing with you, Fauna. But I still say that first we should figure out the best way to do it."

Bwoonhiwda walked to the Baron. She studied him for a moment, then thumped her spear on the floor and declared, "We must act quickwy. If we do not, this man is going to die."

Hulda clutched at her heart. "Why do you say that?"

"Because he is twapped in a magic sweep."

"Sweep?"

"Sweep, sweep!" Bwoonhiwda scowled as if thinking, then bellowed, "Not awake!"

"Why will that kill him?" Hulda cried, her face twisted with grief.

"If we cannot wake him, he cannot eat. If you cannot eat, you die! So this man must wake oah pewish!"

To my surprise Igor began waving his bear in excitement and bellowed, "Igor got idea!"

*The goblins of Nilbog have no bigger friend than Bonecracker John.
This is literally true, because of his great size. It is even more true
because of his great heart.*

—Stanklo the Scribbler

FOLLOW THE BUTTPRINTS

Clutching his bear to his chest, Igor said, "Igor remember time long back his friend Bonecracker John say,
'Igor, one day that toad will be big trouble.'"

"Who's Bonecracker John?" I asked.

"A old giant Igor friends with."

"He's the one who bwoke Sih Mohtimeh!" Bwoonhiwda cried.

Igor chuckled. "That John!"

Karl sighed. "Giants don't exist. They're made-up
stories."

Bwoonhiwda flipped up her spear so swiftly, I didn't
see it happen. Pressing the point to Karl's chest, she
said, "Ah you saying I'm wying, or just that I'm stupid?"

83

"Don't mind Karl," Igor said. "He smart, just not smart as he think he is. Igor say, visit Bonecracker John. Igor say, get John to tell what he know. Igor say . . . uh, Igor say that good idea." He paused, scowled, then shook his bear at us. "That all Igor got to say!"

"But what about William?" I cried.

"All right, here's a suggestion," said Karl. "Fauna and Igor and anyone else who wants to can take some torches and try to track William. The trail should be fairly easy to follow, but if you lose it, change course and visit the giant. Meanwhile, I'll start my research here to see what I can learn about the toad."

I hadn't expected Karl to say anything so sensible. Even so, I saw a problem. "What if you find something we need to know? How will you tell us?"

Before Karl could answer, I felt Solomon's Collar tingle. At the same time, Werdolphus appeared and said, "I can help with that."

Karl—who couldn't see the ghost—staggered backward at the voice from nowhere.

He almost fell over Igor, who had his bear raised above his head, looking for something to bop.

Bwoonhiwda shrieked, causing several cannon-balls to fall off the mantel.

Herky leaped into my arms and buried his face against my neck.

And Hulda . . . well, Hulda turned toward the voice, shook her partial finger in that direction, and shouted, "You have a lot of nerve showing up after all this time!"

"I've been here all along!" Werdolphus replied.

"Not so that anyone would know it, you haven't!"

"Well, we haven't had an emergency like this before."

"Hulda, can you see it?" Karl asked.

"I am *not* an 'it'!" Werdolphus sniffed. Then he put a hand to his brow and said, "I am a tragic spirit, doomed to haunt these halls."

Then he moaned for good measure.

"He's not an it," Hulda agreed. "And I don't have to see him to know who he is. His voice gives him away. He used to work here, until he got careless and died."

"Cruel, Hulda. Cruel," Werdolphus said.

I was tempted to ask Hulda how the ghost had met his doom, but figured if I did, he would disappear again. Since he had offered to help, I didn't want that to happen. So instead I asked, loudly, the other thing I was wondering about: "How can you hear him?"

Hulda blinked, as if she hadn't realized how odd

it was. Before she could answer, Werdolphus said, "It's one of my ghostly powers."

"And how can you get information to us?" I asked. "I thought you couldn't leave the castle."

"Almost true, but not completely." The ghost drifted over to the cannonballs that lay in front of the fireplace. He pointed to one and said, "If you take along the small cannonball that's second from the right, I will be able to come to you at any time."

"Why would a cannonball let you leave the castle?" Karl asked.

Spreading his arms and making his tragic face, Werdolphus said, "It was the instrument of my demise. I am bound to it as much as I am to the castle."

Hulda snorted but said nothing.

Bwoonhiwda picked up the cannonball. It was black and about the size of a goose egg, though round, of course. She hoisted her right braid. The sphere at the bottom was about the same size.

"No pwobwem," she said.

"You're coming with us?" I asked.

"Natuwaw . . . Of coah . . . Yes!"

"Why?"

"The queen sent me to see about the toad. Wheah it goes, I go!"

86

Her thick fingers moving more swiftly than I would have thought possible, she undid the bottom of the braid, took out the ball that was there, replaced it with the cannonball, and wove that into place. When she was done, her head tilted to the right, pulled down by the weight of the cannonball.

"Dwat!" she said. "Too heavy!"

She studied the remaining spheres, then picked up a highly polished one of about the same size. With more quick movements she used it to replace the ball in her left braid, then said, "Ah! Now I am bawanced!"

"What a woman," murmured Igor, clutching his bear and looking moony-eyed.

"Good," I said. "Let's get going!"

"I think I'll come too," Werdolphus said. "I haven't been out of this place since I died."

I glared at him. "I thought the whole idea was that you would bring us word if Karl found something."

"You might need to *send* messages too. I can move back and forth between the castle and the cannon-ball."

"How fast can you travel?" Karl asked.

Werdolphus made a face, which only I could see. "I'm not sure. I do know that I can zip around the castle much faster now than when I was alive."

"You didn't do *anything* fast when you were alive," Hulda said scornfully.

The ghost stuck out his tongue, which looked particularly odd, given his partly bashed-in head. Fortunately, Hulda couldn't see it, so it made no difference.

We still didn't get out the door immediately. First I had to fetch my coat. Then we had to gather torches. And Hulda insisted on packing provisions. When we finally did set out, we had an argument about who should lead. Bwoonhiwda said she should go first, but I convinced her that I had the most experience as a tracker.

"Aw wight," she agreed at last. "But I pwan to be wight behind you. If twubble comes, get out of the way so I can cwobber it!"

Igor sighed and squeezed his bear.

The final order of travel was me, followed by Bwoonhiwda, with Igor at the rear to handle any attack from behind. Herky couldn't manage to stay in line, of course. As for Werdolphus, he sort of floated along beside us. Since no one else could see him, I was the only one who knew where he was from moment to moment.

"I'm so happy to be out of the castle!" he whispered to me shortly after we set out. "After all those years, I was bored to death."

I decided not to point out that he was dead already.

We tromped over the drawbridge, stepping around the boards the toad had broken while leaping across.

A heavy frost covered the ground. This made me worry about William all the more, since he had not been wearing outdoor clothes when the toad snatched him. I hoped it was warm inside the beast's mouth!

The trail itself was easy to spot. The toad landed hard at the end of each jump, which left a deep buttprint. And the push-off for its next leap left clear prints from its webbed feet. Following these, we were able to move quickly back to Bwoonhiwda's camp.

I had wondered about her traveling in this cold. It turned out she had a large wagon, like a little house on wheels. But something was missing.

"Did the toad frighten off your horses?" I asked.

Bwoonhiwda snorted. "I dwag my own wagon. Keeps me stwong!"

"Igor pull wagon for you," Igor said eagerly.

"I need no man to dwag my wagon!" Bwoonhiwda bellowed.

Igor turned around and hugged his bear. I had never seen him look so sad.

It was at Bwoonhiwda's camp that we hit our first snag. Knowing that the creature had passed through

her camp, she had quickly directed us back there. And the regular marks of the toad's landings had confirmed we were on the right path. The problem now was that we had no idea which way the toad had hopped next.

What made this tricky was the size of its leaps. If we had been following a man, the footprints would have been close together. But the toad's buttprints were twenty or thirty feet apart. So for each new hop we had to scan an arc between twenty and thirty feet away to find where it had landed. Fortunately, a hop had to go in a straight line. Since the toad couldn't hop *through* a tree, the number of directions it might have gone was somewhat limited.

Even so, it was slow work.

Herky was best at finding the spots where the toad had landed. There were three reasons for this. First, he moved more quickly than the rest of us. Second, being so small, he was closer to the ground. Third, his huge goblin eyes were made to see in the dark, so he didn't need a torch the way we humans did. (I'm counting Igor as human, though no one is entirely sure about that.)

To my surprise, even Werdolphus turned out to be helpful. Two or three times he managed to spot the next buttprint by floating high enough that he could scan a wide stretch of ground.

"You see," he sniffed, "there are times when it pays to be dead!"

Once, when I was a little way from the others, I saw a terrified rabbit cowering under a bush. When I knelt and quietly asked the little guy if he had seen a giant toad, he nodded and pointed me in the right direction.

I also got advice from an owl and two hedgehogs.

In each case I did this quietly so I wouldn't have to explain to the others why I could talk to animals.

We had been at it for hours, and the moon was low in the sky, when I heard a suspicious noise behind us.

It was answered by a spooky laugh from ahead.

"Fauna!" cried Herky. "Trouble coming!"

He was wrong. Trouble wasn't coming.

It had arrived.

It is my observation just before young ones become adults they go through a stage that is . . . difficult. This seems to be true for all species. Certainly it is true for the scamps of Nilbog.
— Stanklo the Scribbler

CHAPTER NINE

BWOONHIWDA EXPWAINS

Chanting "Blackstone! Blackstone! Blackstone!" a goblin twice as tall as Herky barreled out of the darkness and leaped at me.

I ducked just in time. The goblin sailed over my head. He landed hard, but that didn't slow him down. Goblins are fairly bouncy. With a wild laugh he rushed back at me. I swung my torch at him. As I did, I saw that he wore a red headband like the goblins who had searched my cottage. Then another goblin jumped me from behind.

I fell, dropping my torch.

From all around I heard more cries of "Blackstone! Blackstone! Blackstone!"

It was clear my friends had fights of their own. I couldn't see Igor, but I heard him roar, "Bop! Bop! Boppity bop bop! Bop them goblins on their top!"

I also heard goblin yowls and saw two go flying through the air.

Bwoonhiwda yodeled, "Hoya hoya ho!" which seemed part song, part battle cry.

I rolled across the ground, wrestling with the goblin who had tackled me. He had orange skin, blazing green eyes, and pointed ears the size of my hands. He had pinned my arms, so I wasn't able to get at my knife. Finally we slammed up hard against a tree, me on my back. From that position I saw a squirrel staring down at us.

"You woke me up!" he complained.

"Could you help, please?" I shouted, counting on Solomon's Collar to make my need clear.

The squirrel raced up the tree, away from the fight. I cursed him for a coward as I continued to squirm in the goblin's grip. I had just given my attacker a solid head-butt when a rain of furry bodies made me realize I had been unfair to the squirrel. The little guy had returned with a couple dozen relatives! The squirrels swarmed over my goblin foe, scratching and biting. Yelping in astonishment, the goblin released me and ran into the night, squirrels still clinging to his head and shoulders.

I scrambled to my feet and looked around. I saw Igor send another goblin flying with a mighty bear-bop, but two more clung to his legs. They tripped him and he fell, roaring in anger.

Bwoonhiwda was spinning in a circle. She moved so fast her braids flew out to the sides. With those cannonballs tied into the ends, it was worth a goblin's life to try to get past them. In fact, I spotted two goblins she had knocked out lying motionless on the ground nearby. But I also saw another goblin dangling in a tree, about to drop onto her head.

Little Herky clung to a goblin's neck, yelping in rage as a second goblin tried to pull him away.

That was when the bear came charging into the clearing. He reared up on his hind legs, stretched out his forelegs, and unleashed the most terrifying roar I had ever heard. Then he pulled one of the goblins off Igor's legs and flung it so far I couldn't see where it landed. He lunged for another.

Yelping in terror, the remaining goblins fled into the darkness, leaving behind the two near Bwoon-hiwda, who were either dead or unconscious.

Igor stopped midbop. He looked at his bear, then at the real bear, then at his own bear again. "Uh-oh," he said.

Bwoonhiwda stopped spinning.

Herky, who had leaped away from the goblin he had been riding, hung upside down from a tree branch.

Werdolphus floated close to the bear, studying his face.

"Do you mind?" growled the bear.

Werdolphus floated backward in alarm.

Clearly, my earlier guess about Mervyn, that animals could see ghosts, had been right.

Turning to me, the bear said, "The squirrels told me you needed help."

I made an awkward bow. "We did indeed. My thanks to you for coming to our aid."

"How could I not, when you wear that collar?"

I felt myself blush and wondered if I should confess that I wasn't supposed to have it. I decided to keep my mouth shut.

As long as I wasn't talking, I wasn't lying.

The others took a step closer.

"Fauna talk to bear?" asked Igor.

It would have been stupid, not to mention dangerous, to lie and say I wasn't. So I simply nodded.

Bwoonhiwda thumped the base of her spear on the
ground. "Pwease say to this hewoic beah that Bwoonhiwda, agent of the Queen of the Fowest of Wondah,
thanks him."

I was surprised. Given the way she had been spinning, I would have thought she would be dizzy, even
throwing up. But she looked as if nothing had happened.

When I repeated her words to the bear, he bowed
to her, then turned to me and said, "Tell the warrior
woman that my uncle was a close friend of the queen's,
and I am glad to be of service."

I translated. The bear smiled, which was somewhat
terrifying, given the size of his teeth. "If you have no
more need of my services, I will be going."

"Wait! Have you . . . have you seen any sign of a
giant toad leaping through the woods?"

"A *what?*"

I sighed and made a quick explanation.

"Ah! No, I didn't see it, but that does explain the
thumping and crashing I heard a while back."

With that, he dropped to all fours and trotted away.

I looked and saw that the two goblins were gone

too. I wondered if they had woken and sneaked away or if their friends had carried them off.

When the bear was out of sight, Igor said, "Fauna know how to talk to bears?"

It was either tell the truth or ignore him, and I didn't think I could get away with that. So I said, "It's this collar, Igor. I got it from Granny Pinchbottom."

He clutched his bear and looked around nervously, as if Granny might be behind any tree. "Fauna brave" was all he said.

We resumed our search.

About the time the sun was rising, I noticed we were stepping around patches of ice. I looked ahead, then groaned.

"What's wong?" Bwoonhiwda asked.

"We've reached Bogfester Swamp. It goes on for miles."

The others gathered beside me. We could see the place where the toad had launched a hop that had carried it into the swamp. The problem was, it could easily have landed on any one of the hummocks that rose here and there ahead of us. But those small chunks of solid ground were separated by twenty feet or more of ice—thin ice covering frigid water that I knew could be waist deep. There was no way we could search in that direction! Anyone who plunged through the ice would freeze to death.

"I thought toads were supposed to slow down when it's cold," I said bitterly.

"We fowwow no ohdinawy toad," Bwoonhiwda replied, thumping down the butt of her spear. It cracked through some ice and sank about a foot into the boggy ground. With a scowl that dared anyone to laugh, she pulled it out.

"Well," said Werdolphus, "guess we'll be visiting Bonecracker John after all."

As it turned out, we had to do something else before visiting the giant . . . get some rest!

I hated the idea—stopping for even a moment felt like betraying William. But as we turned from Bogfester, I found that I was groggy and stumbling. I realized I had never gone to sleep the night before.

The others were not much better off, having had only an hour or two of rest before the uproar with the toad had roused them. Only Werdolphus was not tired.

It was Bwoonhiwda who put the situation into words. "We must sweep!"

"Can't sweep," Igor said. "Got no bwoom!"

It was the first joke I'd ever heard him make. From the look on Bwoonhiwda's face, I thought it might also be his last—in fact, maybe the last time he ever said *anything*. Eyes blazing, the warrior woman snapped, "Ah you making fun of me, you big wug?"

"Uh-oh," Werdolphus whispered.

Igor's eyes widened in alarm. Backing up a step, he said, "Igor not make fun. Igor make joke! Igor want to be friend!" He looked at me helplessly. "Fauna! Tell Bwoonhiwda Igor want to be friend!"

I stepped between them. "Igor didn't mean to insult you, Bwoonhiwda. He's just not very good at, um . . . people stuff."

Bwoonhiwda hoisted a braid. The cannonball at the end of it dangled a foot below her hand, and I could tell she was trying to decide whether to use it to clonk Igor. Finally she said, "Tew the big wug that one moh joke wike that, and I cwack his head open wike an egg! Now wet's go back to the wagon so we can *sweep*."

She turned on her heel and started to retrace the route that had brought us to the swamp. I glanced at Igor. His lower lip trembled, and his face was pulled down in the saddest look I had ever seen. He sighed, tucked his bear under his arm, and started after Bwoonhiwda.

A few minutes later Herky, who was walking in front of me, stumbled and went down. When I ran to him, I realized he hadn't tripped. . . . He had actually fallen asleep while walking! It was all the proof I needed that we truly did have to rest before continuing.

I scooped the little nuisance into my arms and trudged on.

When we reached the wagon, Bwoonhiwda pulled open the door and said, "Cwimb in!"

I blinked at her. "All of us? It's so small, we'll have to sleep standing up!"

Bwoonhiwda laughed. "Come inside and wook."

I climbed the little steps at the back, went through the door, and cried out in wonder. The inside of the wagon was far bigger than the outside. Beautiful paintings hung on the walls. Thick carpets covered the floor. Though there was no fire to be seen, it was pleasantly warm, just as Bwoonhiwda had promised.

"The bedwooms ah at the fah end," she said, climbing in behind me.

"How many rooms does this thing have?"

"Depends on how many we need. It's enchanted."

"How did you get an enchanted wagon?"

"The queen knows a wot of wizahds."

• • •

Bwoonhiwda and I shared a room. The "boys"—Igor and Herky—shared another. Werdolphus, who had no need to sleep, decided this would be a good time to go back and check in with Karl.

I agreed.

When I followed Bwoonhiwda into our room, I saw that it held two beds and a wardrobe. The wardrobe was even bigger than the one in my room in the castle.

I slipped off my coat and boots. Still wearing the rest of my clothes, I climbed between the sheets of one of the beds. It felt good to lie down!

Bwoonhiwda stepped into the wardrobe. When she came out again, she had taken off her helmet and was wearing a long white nightdress. I had wondered if she would unbraid her hair to sleep. She didn't. Instead, she carefully lifted the braids as she climbed into bed, then arranged them so that they dangled over the sides.

The cannonballs made a clunking sound as they hit the floor.

She folded her hands over her bosom and said, "Sweep well, Fauna." Then she called, "Wights out!"

The room went dark.

After a moment I said softly, "Bwoonhiwda, may I ask a question?"

"Cewtainwy."

"Why do you talk the way you do? Are you from another country?"

"No, I just have a *w* pwobwem."

"But you say *w* just fine."

"Yes, I have no pwobwem with *w*. My pwobwem is with *w* and *w*."

"What?" I asked, totally confused.

"You know, *w*, as in 'wabbit' and 'wittiw.' If I see a tiny bunny and twy to say, 'What a nice wittiw wabbit,' it comes out 'What a nice wittiw wabbit' instead of . . . of what I twied to say."

"Ah!" I said, starting to understand.

"My pawents had the same pwobwem. They intended to name me . . ." She paused, and I could tell she was struggling with the word. Finally she said, "They meant to have my name sound diffewent. But when the pwiest asked what they wanted to name me, Motheh said, 'Bwoonhiwda!' So that was what he wote in the Big Book of Names." She sighed. "This has caused many pwobwems in my wife."

"I'll bet."

"Chiwdwen can be vewy cwuel," she added softly.

It was strange to hear this woman, so big and strong, speak this way.

"Thank you for explaining," I said.

"No pwobwem. Now wet's get some west!"

I was asleep and dreaming almost instantly. Unfortunately, the dreams all involved giant toads chasing me through dark caverns.

They ended when I heard William shout, "Fauna! Fauna, can you hear me?"

I opened my eyes. William was standing beside my bed!

To my horror, I could see right through him. And Solomon's Collar was tingling the way it did whenever I saw Werdolphus.

"William!" I cried. "Are you dead?"

When a great heart is hidden in an ugly body, much grief and longing can result. This is a particularly human problem. We goblins are all ugly, and take some pride in it!

—*Stanklo the Scribbler*

CHAPTER TEN

AN UNEXPECTED VISIT

William laughed. "I'm not dead, you goof. I just drank some of that Sleep Walk stuff you brought me from Granny Pinchbottom."

I sighed in relief. "But how did you find us?"

"It was *you* I could find. I think it's that collar. It was like it drew me to you. I bet that's also why you can see me, since from what Granny Pinchbottom told you, I should be invisible when I'm doing a Sleep Walk."

He said something else, but I couldn't understand it because Bwoonhiwda started to snore.

William glanced at the big woman. "Who is *that?*"

"Let's go into the other room," I said. "It will be

easier to talk. I'll explain there . . . *after* you finish telling me your story!"

William nodded, then drifted through the closed door.

I had to open it to follow him.

Once we were in the main room, I said, "If you traveled here from your body, you can lead us back to it, right?"

He shook his head. "I didn't follow any kind of path to get here. I just floated up through rock! *That* was the scariest thing yet! Thank goodness it happened quickly. If it had gone on much longer, I might have lost my mind."

"I think you'd better back up and tell this from the beginning."

"I was awake for only some of it. That dratted toad clonked my head against a tree while it was hopping away from the castle and knocked me senseless. When I finally woke up, we were in the forest. I had a horrible headache, but at least I wasn't in his mouth anymore!"

"Where were you?"

"On the ground between his front legs! He was crouched over me, protecting me."

"From what?"

"Goblins! It was weird. They kept shouting 'Blackstone! Blackstone!'"

I shuddered. "The goblins who searched my cottage were shouting that too. Also the ones who attacked us."

"WHAT?"

Quickly I told him about those incidents, then filled him in on what had happened after the toad had hopped away with him. When I got to the part about the Baron, my voice caught before I could finish.

"What?" asked William. "What's wrong?"

"The Baron is in danger," I whispered. Then I explained about the magical sleep.

William looked sick. "This is my fault! I never should have started reading from that book."

"We were both part of it," I said, not wanting him to take all the blame.

He looked at me. "You didn't see what happened after I started reading, did you?"

"What do you mean?"

"I couldn't stop! It was like something had . . . I don't know . . . taken me over and was using me to read the book out loud. It was the creepiest feeling."

"I wondered why you kept going. That really is creepy. Now tell me what else happened with the goblins that attacked you. Oh! Did they have red headbands?"

"Yeah. How did you know?"

"The goblins who searched my cottage, and the ones who attacked us last night, were wearing them. It's like some kind of uniform. All right. Go on with your story."

"Well, the toad kept whapping the goblins with his tongue. He didn't wrap it around them. Instead, he used it like a superlong arm. It reminded me of Igor with his bear. If the toad whacked a goblin with his tongue, it would go flying. They kept trying to get at us, but after the toad knocked out four of them, the others gave up. They picked up the ones who were down and carried them away."

"And they didn't come back?"

"We moved on."

"Did the toad put you into his mouth again?"

"No. He flattened down and looked at me. I could tell he wanted me to climb onto his back. Since he had protected me from the goblins—and since I had no idea where we were or how to get home—I figured I might as well go with him." He smiled. "It's almost like flying when he makes a jump. Hurts when he lands, though. And I have to hold on tight. We're in a cave now, pretty far underground."

"In Nilbog?"

"I don't know. The toad is asleep. He put himself in front of the entrance to block it. Whether he did that to keep me in or keep goblins out, I have no idea. After he dozed off, I decided it was time to try a Sleep Walk."

"Did you come straight here?"

"First I tried to investigate where I was. Turns out I can move really fast this way, and it's not tiring at all. But I couldn't figure out much because there's almost no light, just a little of that glowing fungus. The good thing is, I could always sense where my body was, so I wasn't worried about getting lost."

"You haven't been out too long, have you? Remember, you've got a two-hour limit. If you pass it, you won't be able to get back in."

"Oh, I remember." He reached into his pocket and pulled out the watch the Baron had given him. "I'm using this to keep track."

I smiled. "Good thing your clothes and stuff come with you."

"Definitely better than floating around naked!" he agreed. Then he shook his head. "Karl was right. We should have left that book alone!"

I wanted to deny this, but clearly it was true. To change the subject I said, "Are you scared?"

William looked as if this was the stupidest question he had ever heard. "'Terrified' would be more like it! What's weird is that being out of my body seems to help."

"Really? Going on a Sleep Walk sounds pretty scary to me."

"It is. But not being in my body means I don't feel the things you usually do when you're frightened." He held out his hands. "See? No trembling. And my heart isn't pounding. So my body—or whatever you would call what I am right now—isn't *acting* like I'm afraid. And that helps me stay calm. " He looked down at his see-through self. "Wish I could say the same for my brain. Part of it is screaming." He paused, then said, "I can't tell for sure, Fauna, but I think the toad is frightened too. I wish I had that collar of yours. Then maybe I could talk to him and figure out what's going on."

While I was trying to beat down a flash of guilt, he looked at his watch again. "Yow! I'd better get going!"

"William!" I said as he started to disappear.

"Yes?"

"I'm glad you're alive!"

"Me too. And thanks for looking for me!"

With that, he was gone.

When I returned to the room I shared with Bwoon-hiwda, the sound of her snores almost knocked me backward. I had been lucky enough to fall asleep before that racket had started, but I didn't think I could go back to sleep while it was going on. So I gathered my blankets and dragged them into the main room to make a bed on the floor.

Since we hadn't gone to sleep until almost dawn, it was late when we woke. When I stretched and sat up, a snooty voice said, "I thought you were going to sleep forever!"

Werdolphus had returned.

"Any news from Karl?" I asked.

The ghost shook his head. "Library man has come up dry so far. But he sends his greetings."

"How about the Baron?"

"No change. He hasn't gotten any worse, which is good. But they still can't wake him. Hulda is keeping watch by his bedside. She's really frightened for him."

I felt a twinge of guilt. To change the subject I asked, "How long did it take you to make the trip?"

"How should I know? I had no way to time it."

"Do you want to try? I've got a watch."

"All right. Could be fun. Mark the time. I'll head for the castle and be back as soon as I can."

I took out the watch and flipped open the top. "Ready? GO!"

Werdolphus vanished . . . and returned in less than two minutes.

"Even I am impressed," he said when I told him the time. "But it took a lot out of me. First time I've felt tired since I died!"

Bwoonhiwda called me to breakfast. I had been annoyed when Hulda insisted we wait for her to pack some food before we set out, but now I was glad of it. Having to hunt for our meal would have slowed us down. Even with the food at hand, it was late afternoon before we got moving.

When it was time to start, Igor said, "Igor help pull wagon!"

Bwoonhiwda snorted. "You would just swow me down!"

Igor's face crumpled, and he looked like he was going to cry.

Bwoonhiwda sighed. "Sit on top and give diwections! Wemember, you ah the onwy one who knows the way to the giant!"

"Igor good direction giver!" he crowed as he scrambled up the ladder on the side of the wagon. He positioned himself where a driver would usually sit. I followed him up, as did Herky. Werdolphus, of course, just floated along as he pleased.

Bwoonhiwda started out at a walk. That was impressive enough, considering that she was pulling the wagon with all of us on it. But once we came to the road, she took off at a fast trot.

The road wound through the forest. The afternoon sun was bright on the leaves, which were a wild mix of red, orange, and yellow. The only sound was the thud of Bwoonhiwda's boots. The air was crisp with the smell of autumn. If I hadn't been so worried about William, the ride would have been quite nice.

But I was, so it wasn't.

It did help to know he was still alive, or at least had been a few hours before. But there was no telling what the toad—or the goblins—might do if we couldn't rescue him. I wanted to move faster! Still, I knew we were going faster than we would have on foot.

Herky couldn't sit still for long, of course. Soon he was climbing up and down the sides of the wagon, or scampering from side to side on the roof.

"You're going to fall!" I warned him.

"Herky not fall!" he replied cheerfully, just before he tumbled over the edge.

"Bwoonhiwda!" I cried. "Stop!"

She thudded to a halt. "What's wong?"

"Herky fell off!"

Bwoonhiwda sighed. "Bettah go get him."

I would have thought she would welcome a chance to rest, but she sounded annoyed.

I climbed down from the wagon and ran back toward Herky. When I saw that he wasn't moving, panic surged through me.

"Herky!" I cried. "Herky, are you all right?"

Nothing. Not even a groan.

I knelt beside the little annoyance and put my ear to his chest. He wasn't breathing! I reached into my pocket and pulled out the ball of blue goo, then broke off a glob and shoved it into his mouth.

I heard something beside me, and realized Igor was there. "Herky all right?" he asked, squeezing his bear nervously.

"I don't know, Igor."

As I spoke, the little goblin's eyes fluttered open and he spit out the goo.

"Herky all owiee!" he moaned.

"I told you to hold still," I answered sharply, feeling

113

free to be angry now that I knew he was all right.

"Stinky girl," he whimpered, even as he held out his arms for me to pick him up.

I carried him back to the wagon, opened the door, and shoved him in.

"Stay here," I ordered.

"Girl mean!"

"Girl in a hurry. We have to find William. What if you slow us down again and something bad happens to him because we didn't get there soon enough?"

Herky's eyes widened. He nodded that he understood.

When I climbed back to the top of the wagon, I called to Bwoonhiwda that we could start again. As I settled in beside Igor, I noticed he was clutching his bear more tightly than usual.

"What's the matter?"

"Won't tell?"

"Cross my heart," I said, doing just that.

"Igor want to be Bwoonhiwda's friend. She so beautiful and strong, it make Igor's heart hurt. But Igor don't know how to do it!" He looked at me, and I saw tears in his eyes. "Fauna know how?"

"Sorry, Igor. I don't know much about making friends either."

After that we rode in silence until I said, "How much farther to John's cave?"

Igor pointed to the left. "See mountain? That where old Bonecracker live."

It was hard to tell how far away the mountain really was, but about an hour later Igor called, "Bwoon-hiwda! Stop. Road go wrong way now. Have to walk."

Bwoonhiwda thudded to a halt. She was breathing heavily but other than that showed no sign of the fact that she had been hauling a heavy wagon for hours.

Igor scrambled to the ground. "Got to go that way," he said, pointing into the woods.

"Aw wight," said Bwoonhiwda. "But we have to hide the wagon." Looking up at me, she called, "Fauna! Stand in the woad and wet me know when you can no wonger see us."

I climbed down and watched as she guided the wagon through the trees.

"That's it!" I called when she was out of sight.

"Good! Now come quickwy."

Following her voice, which probably could have been heard back at the castle, I soon saw the wagon again. I scurried to join them. With Igor leading the way, we moved deeper into the forest.

Darkness was falling by the time we reached the mountain.

"See!" Igor said, pointing up. "John's cave!"

Several hundred feet above us was a glimmer of light.

Feeling nervous, I said, "Igor, just how big is this giant?"

"Fauna afraid?"

I wanted to say no but couldn't with the collar on. So I just said, "Maybe a little."

The collar tingled but didn't tighten.

Igor scowled. "Don't be afraid!"

"So you're saying John is perfectly safe?"

Igor shook his head. "No! Saying don't be afraid! It dangerous! John mostly safe, but he got a problem."

"What, exactwy, is his pwobwem?" Bwoonhiwda asked.

"Fear make John hungry. Make him want to eat you. SO DON'T BE AFRAID!"

I had never heard anything less likely to take away fear!

"Can we just get going?" Werdolphus asked.

Given that he was already dead, he didn't need to worry about the giant eating him.

I shook my head. "You still didn't answer my question, Igor. How big is John?"

Igor made his thinking face, then said, "*Very* big!"

As if that had actually told me anything, he started up the slope. We followed, but he moved so quickly, it was hard to stay with him, especially since he kept leaving the path to climb straight up some of the rocky places.

About twenty feet below the mouth of the cave, he paused to wait for the rest of us to catch up. When we were close, he said, "Wait while Igor tell John we coming. Not good to surprise him!"

We watched him scramble the rest of the way to the cave's entrance, then disappear into the mountain.

Soon we heard a deep, rumbling sound that I realized must be John's voice.

Igor reappeared in the rim of light at the cave's mouth. Waving his bear, he called, "John say come visit!"

Werdolphus simply floated up. Herky climbed swiftly over the rocks. Bwoonhiwda and I followed the path.

I was the last to enter the cave.

When I did, I blinked in astonishment.

CHAPTER ELEVEN

THE SPELL OF STONELY TOADIFICATION

I had expected John's home to be a crude stone chamber. But I found myself in a room so elegant, it would not have looked out of place in the Baron's castle.

Lit by torches that neither smoked nor flickered, the cave was lined with shelves . . . and the shelves were crammed with thick books nearly as tall as me. Beautiful rugs woven with intricate patterns covered the floor. A tapestry showing a unicorn in a deep green forest hung on one wall. A statue of a small dragon stood off to the right, next to a bubbling fountain.

In the center of the cave stood a big desk, and by "big" I mean that the top of it was well above my head.

Behind that desk sat Bonecracker John.

I had braced myself for an enormous brute. John was huge, all right. But he was also very old, very slender, and mostly bald. His thin mustache drooped nearly to the floor and was more than twice as long as Bwoonhiwda was tall. His pale blue eyes peered at us through spectacles that had lenses bigger than dinner plates.

"This Bonecracker John!" said Igor, so proud you would have thought he had created the giant himself.

John sighed, causing a small gust of wind. "I wish you wouldn't call me that, Igor."

His voice was deep, and it was obvious he was whispering. I figured if he spoke at his regular level, it would be deafening.

Igor bopped John's foot with his bear. "Who crack Sir Mortimer's bones? John, that who! That why you Bonecracker John!"

John looked at the rest of us. "Igor is referring to an unfortunate incident from long ago. Sir Mortimer accused me of devouring cattle and stealing young maidens. This was a horrible falsehood. Though he claimed to be the bravest of all knights, when I picked him up to discuss the matter, he was overcome with intense fear. This was very bad, due to a certain problem that I have."

"Scared people make John hungry!" Igor crowed, hugging his bear. "Tell them! Tell them what Bonecracker John did next!"

John sighed again. "I, er, threw Sir Mortimer away."

"Stupid Sir Mortimer went long way away!" agreed Igor.

"It was either throw him or eat him," John said. "So really, I saved his life. Alas, very few people understand that. It happened over two hundred years ago, but I've been known as Bonecracker John ever since."

"That because Sir Mortimer got cracked arm, cracked leg, cracked foot, and cracked head," put in Igor.

"I didn't mean to do it!" John roared, his voice rising so that it hurt my ears.

"Stupid Sir Mortimer had it coming," Igor muttered, hugging his bear and looking embarrassed.

John scowled at him.

Igor hugged his bear even closer and glanced at Bwoonhiwda. She didn't look at him—her eyes were focused on John. "Pwease expwain what you know about the stone toad," she said.

"I beg your pardon, but I have no idea who you are."

Igor bopped himself on the head with his bear,

something I had never seen him do before. "Igor forgot manners! Now Igor do introductions. This Fauna. She cranky, but Igor like her. This little goblin Herky. He naughty, but we like him. Werdolphus here, but you can't see him, because he dead." Face lighting up, he finished with "Beautiful lady is Bwoonhiwda."

Bwoonhiwda snorted. I was afraid she might clonk him.

"Thank you," John said. "I assume you asked about the stone toad because it recently came to life?"

"How did you know that?" I asked.

John spread his hands, which were longer than Herky was tall. "When an enormous stone toad goes crashing through the forest, the forest-dwellers tend to notice. Word got to me pretty quickly. I assume that is why you came, since I couldn't think of any other reason for such an odd visit. Happily, you made a good choice. I do indeed know the origins of the toad."

"See!" Igor crowed. "Told you John would know!"

"It's an old family story having to do with my father's cousin Harry. Sweet fellow but not, er . . . well, not very bright."

"John bright!" Igor said.

"Not that bright, Igor, or I would have figured out

where *you* came from by now. However, I can tell you Harry's story. I wrote it down several years ago."

John stood and went to one of the shelves. He pulled out a book bound in red leather.

"Where do your books come from?" I asked, yelling a bit to be heard.

"No need to shout, Fauna. With ears as big as mine, I can hear a cricket fart. As for the books, I make them myself. Have to. Regular books are too small for me to read." He ran his fingers along the shelf. "These contain stories and true events I've written down over the last few centuries. Some are copies of smaller books. I wrote them out by hand so I could read them."

"If you can't read the small books, how can you copy them over?" Werdolphus asked.

"I have friends read them to me."

Igor said sadly, "Igor want to read books to John, only Igor can't read. It a problem."

"It's all right, Igor. You've brought me many fine stories."

Returning to his desk, he opened the book. The pages were almost the size of my cottage door. He flipped through several, then said, "Here we go! 'The Foolish Giant.'"

He began to read. I had often heard people tell

stories, but this was the first time I had heard anyone read one. It was different, but I liked it.

It was about a giant named Harry who was friendly, brave, and kind. Unfortunately, as John had said, he was not very bright. Harry kept getting into trouble because when he tried to be helpful, he made silly mistakes. And because he was so big, his mistakes were big too—big and sometimes very damaging. For example, he once picked a bouquet for the mayor's wife that turned out to be the mayor's best apple trees. The mayor was furious and yelled at Harry to get out of town.

Harry loved the town but couldn't stand to stay where he wasn't wanted. So he packed his things and moved to a cave in the mountains. But one of the children, a boy named Will Smith who was fond of Harry, followed to see where he went.

I thought it was nice that the boy had the same first name as my friend. Also, the story was sounding oddly familiar. I got distracted wondering where I might have heard it, then realized I had stopped listening, and pulled myself back to attention.

As it turned out, sending Harry away was a big mistake. What the mayor had not realized was that a wicked wizard lived in a tower on a hill nearby and wanted to take over the town. The wizard hadn't dared to make trouble while Harry was there, but now that he was gone, the wizard figured he could do whatever he wanted.

He started by turning the mayor's wife into a cow.

"Igor love that part!" cried Igor, hugging his bear in delight.

John peered over the rim of his glasses and waited for Igor to settle down before he said, "The Spell of Total Cowliness only lasted three hours. But it proved what the wizard could do. So when he marched into the town and ordered the people to bring him half of everything they owned or he would turn them into stone toads, they knew he could do it. Grumbling and angry, but also terrified, they gave him what he wanted.

"'Alas,'" read John, "'the wizard was greedy. He kept asking for more, and more, and more. When the people finally ran out of things to give him, he got so mad, he said that unless they brought more by sunset, he would throw the Spell of Stonely Toadification at them!'"

"This scary," muttered Herky. He was clinging to the edge of my coat and had his thumb in his mouth.

John continued. "The townspeople huddled in their homes, waiting for the end. The only one who didn't give up was Will Smith. He went to get Harry. When he made it to the cave, he found Harry sitting on a boulder, shaving. Will gasped out what the wizard was about to do. Harry didn't even finish shaving. He dropped his razor, picked up Will, and ran for town. Soap flew over his shoulders like runaway clouds. His shaving mirror, which was tied around his neck with a leather band, flapped up and down. Will bounced in his pocket until his eyes were going around in circles.

"'Harry reached the town just as the sun was about to set. Time was nearly up. Desperate, he did the only thing he could think of. He set Will on top of a house, then went to stand in front of the town.'"

I gasped. "Why did he do that?"

John smiled. "My good-hearted cousin figured that since he was such a foolish giant, no one would care if he got turned to stone. So he decided to let the magic hit him instead of the town. He may have been weak of brain, but he was strong of heart."

He began to read again.

"'Will shouted for Harry to come back. When the people heard him, they peeked out their windows to see what was happening. They shouted for Harry to come back too. But my father's cousin was determined to protect them.'"

"So Harry is the stone toad," I said.

Lowering the book, John shook his head. "Not at all. What happened next was amazing. When the wizard threw his magic, it hit Harry's big shaving mirror, which reflected the magic straight back to the tower. It struck the evil wizard and turned *him* into one big stone toad."

"YAY FOR HARRY!" cried Herky.

"So *that's* the stone toad that has been in the castle all these years?" I asked.

"How many giant stone toads do you think there are, Fauna?" Werdolphus said with a snort.

I wanted to smack him. Unfortunately, there's not much point in smacking a ghost.

John looked in the direction of Werdolphus's voice. "Fauna's question is a fair one. There's enough magic in the world that there could be more than one of the things. But, yes, the toad I just told you about is indeed the one that resided in the castle. A group of magicians called the League of Teldrum carried it to the Baron's father for safekeeping. They believed there was some danger the spell might eventually wear off. Alas, time has a way of dimming memories. After a while people forgot why the toad was there. And now . . ."

"Now the spell didn't wear off, but William and I brought this evil wizard back to life anyway," I said softly.

"But he wemains a toad," Bwoonhiwda pointed out.

"The question is, *for how long*?" said John. "Wherever that toad has gone, I am certain he is trying to find a way to regain human form."

This idea terrified me. If the toad turned human again, William would be in his clutches. "Just how bad was this wizard?" I asked.

John shook his head. "The problem is less how bad he was than how bad he might become. Some people believe what he really sought in the village was the Black Stone of Borea."

"What's that?" Werdolphus asked.

John scowled. "As you may know, some amount of magic is innate in everything. From pebbles to people, teapots to trees, this is the nature of the world. In the hands of a wizard who knows how to use it, the Black Stone can pull in that magic so that the wizard's power becomes enormously magnified. But when the stone takes the magic from a living creature, whether it be ant or bird, bee, bear, or human, something within that creature goes dead, leaving it in the wizard's control."

I felt a chill shudder through me. John must have seen the look on my face, because he said, "What is it, Fauna?"

"A couple of days ago goblins searched my cottage. They kept shouting 'Blackstone! Blackstone!' When I told Granny Pinchbottom about it, she guessed they were working for someone named Lord Blackstone. Could they have been looking for this Black Stone of Borea instead?"

"Possible, but why in the world would they think it might be in your cottage?"

"I have no idea! This is the first time I ever heard of the thing."

Or was it? Something about the name was nagging at the back of my memory.

John pulled on his lower lip. "Did the goblins say anything else?"

"Yes. When they couldn't find it, they said someone named Helagon was going to be unhappy. Granny got upset when I told her that. Oh, and that same name, Helagon, was on the pedestal under the stone toad."

John started back, almost falling off his chair. Then he put his head in his hands. "This is worse than I imagined," he groaned. "By itself the stone is not a threat to normal people. In fact it is actually a greater threat to magic-makers."

"Why is that?" Werdolphus asked.

"The stone does not absorb magic unless it is being used by someone who can control its power. That's because a person's magic is usually locked away. But if someone has opened the path to his or her magic, as wizards and witches must do, the stone will suck that magic right out if the magic-user does not know how to block it. Only the most powerful of wizards can survive the presence of the Black Stone. But in the hands of one who *does* have the strength and skill, one who knows the stone's secrets and how to use them, the Black Stone of Borea is possibly the most dangerous thing in the world. Helagon, alas, is such a one. And it's not just that he is powerful."

"What do you mean?" I asked.

"Something is broken inside him. He is cruel for the sake of being cruel and delights in causing misery. There is a kind of mystery about him, as no one is sure where he came from, or why he has lived for so long. For him to hold the power of the Black Stone would be a terrible thing."

"So is Helagon the evil wizard who got turned into the stone toad?" I asked.

John shook his head. "No, that doesn't make sense. He couldn't have had goblins out looking for the Black Stone if he was made of stone himself. Besides, he's too smart to be caught that way. Can you think of anything else that might be a clue, Fauna?"

"Yes. The toad has gone underground, possibly to Nilbog."

"How could you possibly know that?" Werdolphus demanded.

"Because I had a visit from William last night."

The others gasped, and realized I had made a huge mistake by not mentioning this earlier. Bwoonhiwda pounded the butt of her spear on the floor, and the fury in her eyes made me think the warrior woman was about to pick me up and squash me.

Fortunately, just then a bell rang.

"Ah," said John. "A message!"

Darkness has a special beauty all its own. However, keeping your friends in the dark about things can lead to bad feelings and crankiness.

—Stanklo the Scribbler

CHAPTER TWELVE

DOWN WE GO

The interruption was enough to keep Bwoonhiwda from throttling me. But as she took a step back, Igor said, "Why Fauna not tell Igor about William?" and the hurt in his voice made me feel even worse than I did already.

What made me feel worst of all was that I realized it was a good question for which I had no good answer. I suppose it was just that I had for so long trained myself to keep my secret that now I kept almost everything to myself. But I couldn't explain that to the others without making them want to know what my secret was. And I couldn't make up a reason, because the collar would strangle me. So I just shook my head and mumbled, "Sorry."

Bwoonhiwda thumped her spear on the cave floor again but seemed at a loss for words.

"I don't understand," Werdolphus said. "If William came back, why didn't he stay? Why are we still looking for him?"

So I had to explain about the Sleep Walk potion, and tell them everything William had said. When I finished, Herky tugged at the edge of my coat and asked in a small, frightened voice, "Butterhead boy all right?"

"He's safe for now, but frightened." Hoping to turn attention elsewhere, I said, "Didn't you say you had a message, John?"

"Yes! I got so distracted by your story, I forgot. I'd better see what it is."

He went to the cave's back wall and opened a small wooden door set in the stone. He reached in and pulled out a lizard. It was fairly big as lizards go, but still smaller than John's little finger. I wondered if the lizard was going to talk to him, then noticed it was wearing a harness. Wrapped in the harness was a roll of paper.

"Fauna, would you take out the message, please?" John said, handing the lizard to me.

I placed the lizard on a footstool. Well, it was a footstool for John. It came up almost to my chin.

"Are you all right?" I asked the lizard as I set it down.

"I'm fine. But I'm glad you'll be taking the message off my back. John is very gentle, but his hands are so big they scare me."

"Fauna, are you talking to that lizard?" asked John. He didn't sound startled, simply curious.

"Fauna got special collar!" Igor said. "It let her talk to animalses and things."

"How did the lizard get here?" I asked, mostly to change the subject.

"Grapevine," John replied.

"I beg yoah pahdon?" said Bwoonhiwda.

"It's a direct connection to Nilbog. One of the goblins—they're very clever, you know—laced together an enormous number of grapevines to make something like a rope. He ran it through a series of flaws in the rock, then looped it back. Now when King Nidrash wants to send me a message, he straps it to a lizard's back, and a pair of goblins turn the cranks that move the vine."

"He makes it sound easier than it is," the lizard muttered. "Those vines go through some pretty tight spots. I was lucky not to lose any skin."

"Perhaps you should look at the message," Werdolphus said. "Just a suggestion, mind you. But who knows . . . might be important."

I unfolded the message and handed it to John. He raised it far above my head to bring it close to his eyes.

"Oh, my," he murmured as he read. "Oh, my. Oh, my!"

Bwoonhiwda thumped the butt of her spear on the cave floor again. "Wet us know what it says!"

"Oh! Oh, yes, of course," said John, sounding flustered. "Here, I'll read it to you.

'My Dear Friend,

The king has asked me to update you regarding new developments in Nilbog. As you may have heard, the stone toad that once rested in the Great Hall of the castle where we were held captive (cursed forever be its name) has come to life. I have shocking new information about the creature but no time to write it down now. Mostly what I want you to know is that if our friends who are seeking the toad come your way, you should speed them on their journey. (Yes, this means you may allow them access to the tunnel in your cave.) There is someone here they need to meet. I will not use her name, for it would be dangerous right now.

In other news, our concern about the scamps grows worse — '"

"What are scamps?" I asked.

John lowered the paper. "That's the word goblins use for those who are no longer children but are neither fully adult. It's a difficult age, both for the scamps and for those around them."

He returned his eyes to the letter and continued reading.

"In the last week another ten have gone missing. Families are in a state of shock and panic and are demanding the king do something. But what can he do when young goblins simply up and depart? Also, there have been odd reports of scamps wearing red headbands being spotted in the outer regions of Nilbog. We do not know who or what is luring them away.

These are perilous times.

Your friend,
Stanklo"

"We've run into some of those red headband goblins," I said. "It wasn't pleasant. But who's Stanklo?"

"The king's scribe and record keeper. He is an old friend of mine. Now, though you must indeed head for Nilbog, I am concerned that the trip may be more dangerous than I expected. Who knows what these prowling scamps are up to?"

"Makes no diffewence!" Bwoonhiwda said. "Wheah the toad has gone, we must go. And pwomptwy!"

John wrinkled his brow. "Pwomptwy?"

"Fast! Soon! Wight away!"

Bwoonhiwda was right. Little as I wanted to return to Nilbog, especially with rogue bands of scamps on the loose, that was where we had to go, and as quickly as possible.

Everyone started talking, a jumble of words that John stopped by using what I can only call his giant voice.

"Cease this babble!"

We fell silent.

Lowering his voice, John said, "Happily, you can make your way to Nilbog from my cave. That should shorten your journey."

Werdolphus said, "I should go back to tell Karl what's going on, and find out if he's learned anything. I'll see you soon."

With that he vanished, though I was the only one who saw it happen, of course.

I turned to John. "How do we get to Nilbog from your cave?"

He went to the back of the cave and slid aside a bookshelf. Behind it was a dark opening.

"This tunnel leads to an entrance to the goblin world. You'll need torches for the first part of the journey, as there will be no light at all until you draw close to Nilbog. It shouldn't take long to make them. Get some branches and I'll let you have an old sock to cut up. You can soak the strips of sock in lamp oil and wrap them around the branches. A few of those should be enough to get you to where the glowing fungus begins."

Igor and I hurried down the slope to gather branches. When we returned, John brought out the sock he had promised. It was so big, I could have fit inside it and the smell made me stagger back. I wasn't sure we needed to soak the thing in oil . . . I was afraid it might explode the moment we tried to light it!

Holding my breath, I took out my knife and began to slice the sock into long strips.

"Here's the oil," said John, setting down a cup so big I could have taken a bath in. I dipped the pieces of sock into the oil, then wound them around the branches.

When the torches were ready, we assembled at the

entrance to the tunnel. I handed a torch to Bwoon-hiwda, kept one for myself, and passed the rest to Igor. The plan was to use two torches at a time. I had wanted to use only one, to make them last longer, but Bwoon-hiwda pointed out that if that one died unexpectedly, we would have no way to light another.

John said he was "fairly sure" we had enough torches to reach Nilbog. I wasn't happy about that. I would have preferred "absolutely positive."

When we were ready, the giant used a candle the size of my leg to light our first two torches. Bending down, his enormous face wrinkled with concern, he said, "I wish you good fortune on your journey, for all our sakes."

"Does the tunnel go straight to Nilbog?" I asked, looking at the opening ahead of us. The light from our torches reached only twenty or thirty feet in. After that, all was darkness.

"No, you will find many turns and twists. However, they should all be marked."

"Don't matter!" cried Herky, bouncing up and down. "Herky can find the way! Herky will show! Herky good little goblin!"

I wasn't sure how long the little menace could manage to be good, but I kept my mouth shut except to say good-bye to John.

• • •

Entering the earth is both fascinating and frightening. I like being in a place that so few people have seen. I like the coolness. I like the moist-rock scent of the air. I like the way the walls of the tunnels are sometimes smooth, sometimes rough and jagged, sometimes slick with dripping water.

What I *don't* like is coming to places where a tunnel opens to become a cavern so enormous that the light of a torch can't reach the far side, or even the roof above you. Those spots are even worse when you reach a split in the cavern floor and have to cross it on a narrow stone bridge. Usually you can't see how deep the gap is, or how sturdy the bridge might be. The only good thing about the big caverns was that the smoke from our torches could float away. In the low, narrow tunnels it was trapped and made us cough.

I don't know how long we had been traveling when Bwoonhiwda's torch sputtered and went out.

Igor handed me a fresh torch. I lit it from mine and passed it to Bwoonhiwda.

We walked on.

About five minutes later my own torch went out.

I lit a new one from Bwoonhiwda's.

Occasionally I would check my watch, which I had

decided was more useful than I had first expected.

Each torch was lasting about half an hour. When we were down to our last four, Bwoonhiwda said, "Wet's onwy use one now."

"But you said we'd be in trouble if it goes out," I objected.

"Twue. But even biggeh twubble if we use them up befoah we weach the gwowing fungus!"

That was true enough.

"All right," I agreed. "One torch."

Now that Bwoonhiwda had put the worry in my mind, I began to fret that the last torch would go to ash too soon and leave us in the dark.

On the surface world I don't mind darkness that much. Up there you know that sooner or later the sun will rise. Underground, darkness is forever. And being caught in that total darkness was starting to seem more likely—and more terrifying.

I glanced at the others. Igor and Bwoonhiwda looked as grim as I felt. The only one who didn't seem concerned was Herky, who kept bounding ahead, then scampering back. The fourth or fifth time he did this, he scurried to me and clambered into my arms. "Herky scared!" he whispered.

"Because of the dark?" I asked.

He shook his head, causing his ears to flap against my face. "Not the dark. The noises!"

"What kind of noises?"

"All *sssss, sssss, sssss!*"

I didn't like the sound of that.

"Is there any other way to Nilbog from here?" I asked.

He shook his head again and pressed his face to my neck.

Tightening her grip on her spear, Bwoonhiwda whispered, "Move quietwy and be weady for anything!"

I knew that whatever was ahead, Bwoonhiwda would be the first to face it. I knew Igor would fight like a madman to protect us. However, I also knew that we were deep underground, in a narrow tunnel, with only a single torch for light.

It was not the happiest moment of my life.

We moved on as silently as possible.

Soon I heard it too . . . a constant low hissing. I started to speak, but my words were drowned out by a burst of fluttering.

Bwoonhiwda shouted in anger as she dropped her torch.

The flame died, plunging us into complete darkness.

That was when I felt tiny claws dig into my neck.

Though it made life safer when they left, I have always felt the world was poorer for the loss of the dragons.
—Stanklo the Scribbler

CHAPTER THIRTEEN

STERNGRIM

A breeze made by the flapping of small wings rustled my hair.

Bats! I thought. *We've disturbed a colony of bats!*

I was wrong. Whatever had landed on my neck had a long, twisting, snakelike body. It began to climb my head, needle-sharp claws piercing my scalp as it went.

"Stop!" I cried, grabbing for it.

"Why?" asked a soft voice.

I pulled my hand back, startled, then realized I had understood the creature because of Solomon's Collar.

"Your claws are hurting me," I cried, yelling to be heard above the shouts, screams, and bellows of my companions.

"But I need to explore you," it replied, head so close to my ear I felt its hot tongue flick against me. "Need to know what you are."

"I'm a people! What are *you?*"

"Winged lindling."

Around me I heard my friends struggling to fight off the creatures.

"Yike, yike, yike!" That was Herky, shrieking in dismay.

"Don't know what to bop! *Don't know what to bop!*" That was Igor, roaring his fury.

"Hoya hoya ho!" That was Bwoonhiwda, trumpeting her battle cry.

Raising my own voice, I yelled, "Lindlings, stop!"

Nothing happened. I didn't know if it was because they were ignoring me or if they simply couldn't hear me above the clamor.

"I'll stop them," said the lindling who had been on my head. It fluttered away, and I heard it calling to the others to pull back.

A minute or so later the shouting died down. In the near-silence that followed I heard Herky whimper, "Bad things. Bad, bad things!"

"I talked to one," I said. "I think they might be friendly."

"What ah they?" Bwoonhiwda asked.

"Winged lindlings."

"Winged windwings?"

Just then the lindling I had spoken to returned to my shoulder. "Cannot keep them quiet much longer. They need to investigate you. Will start soon whether or not you want them to."

"Will they hurt us?"

"Claws might scratch, but do as I say, and I promise no bites."

I wondered what the promise of a winged lindling was worth, but figured they were going to start again whether or not we agreed.

"What do you want us to do?" I asked.

"Hold still. We must climb on you. Need to learn your shape, find out what you smell like."

I told the others what the lindlings wanted.

"Won't bite?" Herky asked nervously.

"They didn't bite before, did they?"

Herky sighed, but I could tell he wasn't going to argue.

"Everybody ready?" I asked.

When they had all answered, I said to the lindling, "Go ahead."

The creature let out a shrill cry. I felt three more

lindlings land on me. Having those clawed feet and cool, snaky bodies move over me in the darkness made my flesh creep. Without intending to, I squealed. Igor, on the other hand, began to laugh. "That tickle!" he cried. "Stop, things! Don't tickle Igor!"

"Be quiet, you big wug," boomed Bwoonhiwda.

Her great voice echoed around the stony walls: "Wug . . . wug . . . wug."

I tried to hold absolutely still myself, but it wasn't easy. It was only the fear that if I *did* move, it might make the lindlings bite or scratch that kept me from trying to yank them off.

I guess Herky was not able to manage holding still, because I heard him cry, "Ow ow ow ow owicc! Bad critters! Bad, bad critters!"

This was followed by a flutter of wings and some angry hissing. Another of the creatures landed on my shoulder and said, "Little one is a small goblin."

I realized it was talking to the other lindlings, not me.

"Well, we expect goblins down here," said "my" lindling.

"Are you done yet?" I asked.

"I will be back," said my lindling. It made a shrill sound that I understood to mean "Lindlings, gather!" and fluttered away.

• • •

I'm not sure how much time went by before the lindling returned. When you're standing in a pitch-black cave and have just had snakelike creatures crawling all over you, a minute seems to last forever. But finally the lindling returned to my shoulder and said, "We want to know why you are here."

I explained that we were heading for Nilbog to search for a friend who had been kidnapped by a giant toad.

The lindling made a hissing laugh.

"It's not funny!" I said angrily. "My friend is in danger."

"Sorry. But that is the silliest story I have ever heard. And you were bad to disturb our lair with all that horrid light! Despite that, we are willing to let you pass."

"We didn't know you were here. Until now I didn't even know lindlings existed!"

"We are all that is left of the dragons," replied the lindling sadly. "Well, a few of the great ones may still be hiding in the mountains. But mostly they are gone."

"Gone?"

"Earth is not as kind to dragons as it used to be. Most have fled to another world, through doors created by the wizard Bellenmore. We lindlings were left behind . . . too small to be noticed, I guess."

I wasn't sure how to react to this. Though it seemed sad, I found it hard to get upset about a lack of giant, fire-breathing, town-destroying monsters. I decided not to say that. Instead I called to the others, "The lindlings have agreed to let us pass!"

"How can we go on without wight?" Bwoonhiwda asked.

It was a good question. Unfortunately, I didn't have an answer.

The lindling on my shoulder nipped my ear. "What did the big woman say?"

I explained the problem.

The lindling was silent for a moment, then said softly, "I could guide you."

"You wouldn't mind?"

"Actually, I would be glad to get away from the others for a while." Dropping its voice, it added, "I do not really fit in here."

I wondered what it would take for a lindling not to fit in with its herd, or flock, or whatever a group of them was called. But I certainly understood not fitting in. And I couldn't think of any better way for us to go forward.

I explained the creature's offer to the others. They agreed it was our best chance to get to Nilbog now that our torches were out.

"What's your name?" I asked the lindling.

"Sterngrim the Awesome!"

I had to resist laughing. "Isn't that kind of a big name for someone your size?"

"We are dragons!" Sterngrim replied proudly. "We may be tiny in size, but we are mighty in our hearts!"

"With a name like that, I take it you're a male."

"I most certainly am not! I am a female, and far more fierce than my brothers. Do not be rude to me unless you wish to lose an ear."

I promised to be careful, and Sterngrim positioned herself on my shoulder. Actually, she started out on my head, but her claws were like needles in my scalp, and I asked her to move down. Once we had that arranged, we set out, this time with me in the lead.

Because of the total darkness, it was safer to stay connected. So Bwoonhiwda kept her left hand on my shoulder. Herky walked beside me, holding my hand. Igor had to be last, of course, because no one was allowed to touch his hump. Bwoonhiwda had him hold on to one of her braids, but warned him not to pull it or she would clonk him.

We had not gone more than ten steps when Stern-grim said, "Curve coming up!"

I repeated this for the others.

"Keep one hand in front of you," Sterngrim said. I did as she told me. When my hand touched stone, I felt around a bit, then called, "We're turning to the right."

Our progress was slow and frustrating. Twice we had to slide down slick slopes. This was scary because I had no idea how long the slopes were, or what was at the bottom. Also, we had to let go of one another to do it.

It was the same when we had to climb a crumbly patch, which took two hands. Since we were moving in complete darkness, I didn't know when I might suddenly put my hand down on nothing. It happened twice. The second time Bwoonhiwda grabbed my foot just before I went over an edge.

My scream echoed around us for a long time.

The worst moment came when we reached another of those stone bridges. No way was I going to walk across the thing when I couldn't even see it! I got on my hands and knees to crawl, sliding each hand forward to make sure there was always solid stone beneath my fingers. I could hear rushing water below but had no idea if it was five feet down or five hundred.

Finally Sterngrim said, "We have reached the far side."

I crawled forward another several feet before I was willing to stand again. Then we re-formed our line and moved on.

Since I couldn't consult my watch, I have no idea how long we traveled this way.

It felt like forever.

"Narrow ledge!" warned Sterngrim suddenly. "Hug the wall on your left so you don't fall off."

I passed the word to the others, then pressed my back to the wall. I swept my foot sideways before each step to make sure I had a solid place to stand. More than once I could feel where the ledge ended and the drop-off began.

We had been traveling this way for several minutes when a voice next to my ear said, "Boy, it's *really* dark down here!"

I screamed and jumped, nearly falling off the ledge. My scream startled the others, and I heard them cry out too. Fortunately, I didn't hear the long, drawn-out wail of someone falling into an abyss.

"Werdolphus!" I exclaimed. "Next time you're going to do that, warn me!"

"How could I warn you? The only way I could let you know I was here was by talking to you. What did you want me to say? 'Warning, warning, I'm about to say something'? It's not like I sneaked up on you and shouted 'BOO!'" He chuckled at the thought. "Good thing I didn't think of that, or I might have. Would have been pretty funny."

"It probably would have killed me!"

"There are worse things that could happen," the ghost replied.

It was one of those times when, if he hadn't been dead already, I would have been tempted to kill him.

"Fauna all right?" asked Igor.

"I will be when my heart stops pounding."

"I didn't *have* to come back, you know," Werdolphus said, sounding cranky. "I just wanted to bring you a news report."

"Can it wait until after we get off this ledge?"

"I suppose so."

When Sterngrim finally announced that we were on safe ground, I said, "All right. Now you can talk to me."

But before he could speak, Bwoonhiwda said, "What took you so wong? I thought you could come and go instantwy."

"Getting there quickly didn't mean finding Karl quickly. In fact, I didn't find him at all."

"Did something happen to him?" I asked.

"He finally located the information he needed."

"If you didn't talk to him, how do you know that?"

"He left a letter for me. And Hulda filled in the details." He sighed. "It's odd to be dead and watch someone you knew when you were alive get older and older, while you stay the same."

"What letter say?" Igor demanded.

"Turns out you should have brought the book and the mirror with you. According to Hulda, once Karl figured that out, he grabbed his hair and started walking in circles. She said his language was absolutely shocking."

"So why wasn't he there?" I asked.

"Because he packed up the book, strapped the mirror to his back, and set out to find us."

This startled me, and made me wonder if there was more to Karl than I had thought.

"How is he pwanning to find us?" Bwoonhiwda asked. "He has no idea wheah we ah!"

"Actually, he does. When I went back the first time, I told him we were heading for the giant's cave. He acted like that was a crazy idea, of course. But according to Hulda, after I left, he searched the library and found a map showing the way to John's."

"What will he do once he gets there?" I asked.

"How should I know?"

"Well, can't you go back and help him?"

"Of course not. I can only go two places—the castle and wherever Bwoonhiwda is with that cannonball. I have to travel in a straight line between them. I can move around a bit only when I am near one or the other."

Could Karl carry enough torches? Could he get past the lindlings? Could he find the way without a lindling to guide him? It seemed impossible that he could find us. So if we really needed the mirror and the book, we had lost already.

Then I realized I wasn't just worried about the book and the mirror.

I was worried about Karl.

I frowned. I was starting to care about too many people.

Since there was nothing else to do, we started out again. After what felt like a million years, a dim glow appeared ahead of us. At first I wondered if my eyes were so desperate for light that they were imagining it. Then I realized it must be the glowing fungus.

153

As we walked on, the yellow-green light grew more distinct.

"Almost to Nilbog!" Herky whispered excitedly.

Before long I could see the walls of the tunnel.

"Wait here," said Sterngrim. "I want to check on what's ahead."

When she fluttered off my shoulder, I got my first look at a lindling. Her snaky body was as thick as my wrist and almost as long as my arm. She had four short legs, with two bat-like wings sprouting from above the front pair. Her tail switched back and forth as she flew. That was all I could see, though. The light was too dim to make out what color she was, or any small details.

In a moment she was out of sight. I couldn't tell if the light was too low or if she had gone around a curve. As I began to wonder if she had simply abandoned us, I heard a shrill cry.

"Let me go. *Let me go!*"

It was Sterngrim, and she sounded terrified.

I raced forward. I can't say why I cared so much what happened to her. I hadn't known her that long. But she had guided us safely through the dark, so I felt that I owed her something.

There was indeed a curve in the tunnel. Round-ing it, I entered a cave lit by large patches of glowing fungus.

On the far side of the cave, about twenty feet away, was the opening to another tunnel. At the mouth of that tunnel I saw two things in the fungal light.

One was a creature that looked something like a goblin but was much bigger than any goblin should be.

The other was Sterngrim, writhing desperately in the monster's fat-fingered hands.

Never have humans and goblins worked together better and more closely than when we collaborated to seal the Pit of Thogmoth. It was our greatest achievement.

—Stanklo the Scribbler

CHAPTER FOURTEEN

WONGO

I pulled out my knife and rushed forward, crying, "Let that lindling go!"

The creature holding Sterngrim looked at me in surprise. "Why?"

He sounded as if he had gravel in his throat.

Without thinking, I replied, "Because she's my friend!"

I was right in front of him now. He was more than twice my height, dull gray in color, and hairless as the cannonballs that the Baron collected. Though the creature had pointed ears and a nose like a giant potato, up close he looked less like a goblin and more like what he really was: a troll.

Gazing down at me, he laughed. "And why, small and incautious human, should I care that this vermin is your friend?"

"Because she is my knife's friend too!" I said, holding up my blade. I was acting more bravely than I felt, but I had long ago learned that this can be useful in a bad situation.

It didn't impress the troll, though. "Oh," he said mockingly, "that makes all the difference! I quiver in terror at your awesome blade."

I didn't want to stab him if I could avoid it.

So I punched him in the knee.

"*OWWWW!* That was uncalled-for, you oddly aggressive young female!"

"It was compwetewy appwopwiate!" bellowed Bwoonhiwda. I was delighted to see that she and Igor were now beside me. She had one braid in her hand and was twirling it around her head. "Wet that windwing go oh face my wath!"

"Your what?"

"My wath! My wath! My mighty wage!"

"I think she means she's going to clobber you with that cannonball," I explained.

The troll sighed and released his grip on Stern-grim. She fluttered over and landed on my shoulder. I could feel her trembling.

"You strange assortment of people are remarkably nasty," said the troll. "I am simply trying to perform my designated task."

"What task is that?" I asked.

The troll straightened his shoulders. "I am Troll Wongo! With stony fortitude I guard this entrance to Nilbog. No one may pass unless he, she, or it has good reason."

"We got reason!" Igor roared, shaking his bear at the troll. "We got to get William!"

Wongo blinked. "Do you mean *the* William, you odd and hairy personage? The boy hero who released the goblins from their horrid captivity?"

"Yes, *that* William!" I shouted. "I'm his friend."

"Herky William's friend too!" cried the little goblin, darting out from behind Igor.

"Herky and Igor and I were with William when he healed the king," I told the troll. "We all helped."

"That right!" Igor bellowed, waving his bear over his head. "Igor and goblins friends now!"

The troll bowed. "I blossom with apologies. If I had known you were friends of *the* William, I would not have obstructed you. Besides, I didn't realize you had a goblin with you. Anyone with a goblin escort, however small and annoying that goblin may be, is allowed to enter Nilbog. Yet even had I known all this, still would I have apprehended that winged messenger of darkness now perched upon your shoulder. Why in the name of feldspar and granite are you traveling with a pest like that?"

Sterngrim hissed. I wondered if she had understood his words or was simply still angry.

"She's my friend," I repeated. "She guided us through the darkness."

"You cannot be friends with a winged lindling. They are nasty, crawly, mindless vermin spawned in the Pit of Thogmoth."

"That sound bad," said Igor.

"Sterngrim, would you please prove to this troll that we are friends?" I asked.

"What would you like me to do?"

"Why don't you fly over and poop on his head."

"Good idea!"

With a flap of her wings, Sterngrim lifted away. Though the troll couldn't understand her replies, he had certainly understood what *I* was saying. When Sterngrim started in his direction, he wrapped his thick-fingered hands over his bald gray head and shouted, "All right. I believe you! Call the winged menace back!"

"You sure you don't want more proof?" I asked, trying not to smile as Sterngrim circled above him. "I can offer it."

"No, that was sufficient."

Like the troll, Sterngrim could understand only half of what was being said. "What do you want me to do?" she asked.

I motioned for her to return to my shoulder. Once she was back, she whispered into my ear, "Wish you had not stopped me. He had a good head-poop coming."

"I agree. But we still need to get past him."

The troll squatted, which put him at about eye level with us, and asked, "What has happened to *the* William?"

I was surprised by the concern in his gravelly voice.

Quickly I explained how the stone toad had come to life and carried William into Nilbog. I left it at that. I didn't think he needed to know about the Black Stone of Borea. In fact, it seemed better to keep that matter a secret.

Wongo pulled on his big gray lower lip and nodded. "Word of a stone toad of bizarre size entering Nilbog did reach me here at my tragically isolated outpost. However, I was not told that said creature carried *the* William with it. You may pass, of course. However, I feel I should warn you there is trouble in Nilbog."

"What kind of twubble?" Bwoonhiwda asked.

"As you likely know, you obstreperous, warlike, and probably dangerous female, the spirits of the goblins were long imprisoned in Toad-in-a-Cage Castle. When they were released, they were so joyful that at first they overlooked the problems that had overtaken Nilbog during their time of captivity."

"What pwobwems would those be?"

"If you leave a place for over a hundred years, it will decline and decay. It wasn't the goblins' fault they'd been gone, of course, but Nilbog is crumbling. The bridges are weak, and two have fallen. The roads are pitted with holes deep enough to swallow a goblin the size of the one you carry. Even worse, the places where they grow food—the great fungus caverns, the wonderful lizard farms—are in bad shape. The goblins are unhappy. And unhappy goblins are never a good thing. I have heard rumors of young goblins, scamps, prowling the far caverns . . . and more rumors that they have been lured to this by some wicked but compelling person. I will let you pass, but I cannot guarantee your safety if you go on."

"The city was filled with joy just last year," I said. "How could things get so bad so fast?"

Wongo shrugged again. "Anyone who thinks about it would know that these problems grew over a long time, and so will take a long time to undo. But many do not think. Instead, they quiver with impatience and demand that problems be fixed at once, no matter how long they took to develop." He paused, then said softly, "Also, a few of us suspect that the same dark force that has been luring away the scamps is spreading lies and rumors to make things worse."

"That's horrible," I said. "Even so, dangerous or not, we still have to find William."

The troll nodded solemnly. "I agree. You must get *the* William. But do you know where he is? Nilbog is a big place."

"We do not," I admitted unhappily.

Wongo stroked his chin, then said, "Though I hesitate to suggest such a drastic course, perhaps you should pay a visit to Flegmire."

With a cry of despair Herky flung himself forward. He wrapped his arms around Wongo's right leg and burst into tears, wailing, "Noooooo! Don't make Herky go to Flegmire!"

Much as Herky annoys me, I didn't like seeing him so upset. Kneeling beside him, I said, "What's the matter?"

"Flegmire scary," Herky sniffed, his face still pressed to Wongo's leg.

"Why is Flegmire scary?"

Herky turned his big eyes to me. "Herky's momma tell him, 'Herky, don't you go near Flegmire. Not ever!' When Herky ask why, his momma say, 'Because Flegmire eat bad little goblins!' Herky bad. Herky good sometimes, but Herky bad *lots* of times. Herky don't want Flegmire to eat him. So Herky got to stay here."

With a shudder that made his big ears flap, he buried his face against the troll's leg once more.

Wongo burst out laughing.

"What's so funny?" I demanded.

The troll shook his massive head. "Goblin mothers have been telling that story to small and naughty goblins since before I climbed out of my rock."

"But is it *twue?*" demanded Bwoonhiwda.

Wongo wiped some pebbles from his eyes. I figured they must be the troll version of tears of laughter. "Not in the least. Goblin mothers are simply trying to scare their boisterous and overactive offspring into behaving. I don't blame them. For a goblin child, mischief comes as naturally as breathing."

As he said this, Wongo plucked Herky from his leg and held him at arm's length.

"Noooooo!" the little goblin wailed. "Don't wanna go! Don't wanna go! *Herky don't wanna get eated!*"

"Oh, for pity's sake," I said. "Give him to me."

When Wongo passed Herky to me, I held the little agitation in front of my face, looked him in the eye, and said firmly, "I promise I won't let Flegmire eat you."

"Really?"

"Yes. I promise to protect you."

"Herky go if Fauna protect him."

"Just who is this Fwegmiah?" Bwoonhiwda asked Wongo.

"A wise, elderly, somewhat demented goblin who lives on the outskirts of Nilbog. She was the only goblin *not* imprisoned when the others were captured. Unfortunately, a hundred and twenty-one years of solitude drove her a bit mad."

"Can you tell us how to find her?" I asked.

"Follow the tunnel I will now allow you to enter. It

164

will bring you to a ridge that overlooks the city. Do *not* take the path that leads down to the city. Instead, turn right and take the path that runs along the crest of the ridge. After a while you will come to a stone bridge that crosses a waterfall of luminous beauty. On the far side of this bridge the path divides. Take the path less traveled, which slopes down to the right. This will lead you to the mushroom forest."

"Mushwoom *fowest?*" Bwoonhiwda asked.

Wongo shrugged. "When thousands of mushrooms grow as tall as trees, you might as well call it a forest. Anyway, that path will lead you through the mushroom forest to Flegmire's dark and lonely cave."

"Thank you," I said. "May we pass now?"

"Just one more thing. When you speak to Flegmire, you should address her as 'the Wisest of the Wise.'"

"Is she really the Wisest of the Wise?"

"Probably not, but she likes to be called that. And her advice *is* the best you're likely to get . . . especially if she rolls the bones for you. And that slightly unlikely event is more apt to occur if you treat her with respect. Even if she is not really the wisest of all goblins, she is definitely the oldest, and that counts for something."

Having said that, Wongo moved aside so we could enter the tunnel. As I walked past, he said softly, "Good luck, you small, scruffy, but touchingly brave girl. I hope you find your friend."

I thanked him, not admitting I had no idea what we were going to do if and when we did find William.

"Thank you for saving me from that troll," Sterngrim whispered when we were well past Wongo.

I didn't want to make a big deal out of it, so I shrugged and said, "It was nothing."

"Are you saying my life is worth nothing?" she shrieked.

Then she leaped from my shoulder and fluttered away.

I called for her to come back, but got no reply.

That is why I don't like talking. It's too easy to make a mistake. I wondered if I would ever see her again. I had started to like having her with me.

"Sterngrim go away?" asked Igor, sounding puzzled.

"For now. I hope she will come back."

We continued on. At least we could see now, since the tunnel walls were lined with the glowing fungus.

When we reached the end of the tunnel, we found ourselves on a ridge overlooking the city, just as Wongo had said.

I had seen Nilbog City before, but it still amazed me. The goblins had built it in an enormous cavern. The reason the city is visible is that huge amounts of the glowing fungus grow everywhere. The stuff lines the paths that weave among the buildings. Wherever two paths cross, there is a tall pole with the fungus wrapped around it. Whole rooftops are covered with it. However, we also saw large, dark areas that I now understood came from the years of neglect.

Not far to our left roared a huge waterfall. This was not the one Wongo had told us to look for—it was much too wide to be spanned by a bridge. I recognized it from my first trip and realized we must have entered the cavern from the opposite side this time, since when William and I had come here before, that fall had been directly across from us.

The fall plunged over a steep cliff. From its base a river flowed to the center of the city. Rivers and streams ran in from other directions as well, merging to form a large lake at the city's lowest point.

In the center of that lake was an island.

From the center of the island rose Castle Nilbog. It had seven towers, each sticking up at a different angle.

I was glad we were going to skirt the city. Though

the castle was a fascinating place, I didn't want to go back. The memory of being a prisoner in its dungeon remained fresh in my mind.

Stopping to admire Nilbog City turned out to be a bad idea. We were still looking at it when we heard a chant of "Black Stone! Black Stone! Black Stone!" from behind us.

That was all the warning we had before the attack.

Being court scribbler is a solitary life. Most of my time is spent alone, wrestling with words that refuse to behave as I wish them to. On the other hand, I get to be in attendance at great events!

—Stanklo the Scribbler

CHAPTER FIFTEEN

SOPHRONIA

A mischief of headband-wearing scamps had crept up the far side of the ridge. Now they flung themselves at us.

Igor thrashed around him with his bear. "Bop! Bop! Bop!" he roared. "Boppity bop bop!"

Goblins flew in all directions.

Bwoonhiwda didn't have room to spin in a circle the way she did the first time we were attacked. So she just picked up goblins and threw them.

They went a long way.

Herky leaped onto an attacker's leg and chomped down on it. The big goblin howled and tried to pull him off, but Herky clung tight.

Werdolphus began popping up beside goblins and shouting into their ears. His voice, seeming to come from nowhere, distracted and frightened them.

As for me, I pulled out my knife and held it in front of me. The goblins kept a distance from it. But I had nothing to cover my back, and one of them leaped onto me from behind. I fell face-first. He pinned me down, shouting, "The stone! Give me the stone!"

I struggled but couldn't get up. Then I heard a hiss, and the goblin holding me down shrieked in pain.

Sterngrim had returned!

The goblin grabbed at the lindling, who was clawing his head. As he did, I rolled out from under him.

Scrambling to my feet, I saw more goblins racing toward us. I was terrified until I realized these goblins were not wearing red headbands. Shouting "For king and Nilbog!" they plunged into the battle, attacking our attackers. Soon goblins were bouncing and bounding all over. Soon after that the red headband group ran, yelping, into the darkness.

"Thank you for rescuing me," I whispered to Sterngrim, who was once more perched on my shoulder.

"It was nothing," she said. Then she gave my ear a little nip and whapped the back of my head with one of her wings.

The leader of the mischief that had come to our rescue stuck his finger into his nose and nodded, which I took to be some kind of goblin salute. "I am Grickle, leader of the Seventh Mischief and Marching Society. Welcome to Nilbog, Fauna Goblin Friend. Why do you have a winged lindling on your shoulder? Would you like me to kill it for you?"

Glad that Sterngrim couldn't understand him, I said fiercely, "She is my friend!"

Grickle looked at me oddly but went on to greet the others.

"Welcome, Igor Goblin Friend. Welcome, Herky, goblinspawn. Welcome . . . er, welcome, big strong woman."

"Her name Bwoonhiwda," Igor said.

Grickle nodded. "Welcome, Bwoonhiwda."

"Hey, I'm here too," Werdolphus said.

The voice from nowhere caused Grickle to jump, so I had to explain about having a ghost with us. When I was done, I said, "Thank you for driving off those other goblins. Do you know why they attacked us?"

Grickle shook his head. "We don't understand what is happening with the scamps. We've had reports of some going topside, and we have reports of others prowling the outer caverns. But this is the first I know of them attacking anyone. I'm glad we reached you when we did. We were coming to escort you to Castle Nilbog."

I started to ask how he had known we were coming, then realized Bonecracker John must have sent that little messenger lizard back with the news.

"You did arrive just in time," I said. "And we thank you for your help. But we are not heading for the castle. We are on a mission."

The goblin scowled. "You are a Goblin Friend, but that does not give you free rein to wander about Nilbog without first coming to see King Nidrash. He has sent for you, and it would be rude and ungoblin-like not to go."

"You don't understand! We are looking for *the* William. He has been captured by a giant toad."

"The king is aware of that. He is also aware of his debt to William, and to you, and that it is enormous. But he insists you come anyway." He leaned forward and whispered, "There is someone you must meet. I am not free to say who, but I can tell you that the king feels it may help you in your quest."

I sighed. It looked like we would be going to the castle after all.

I hoped I could manage to stay out of the dungeon this time!

. . .

Entering Nilbog City made me sad. The first time I'd been there, I had not fully understood the damage that had occurred during the years of the goblins' captivity. Now that Wongo had explained it, I couldn't help but be aware of the decay that had overtaken Nilbog.

One thing that had not suffered—or perhaps had been repaired already—was the stone bridge that leads from the edge of the underground lake to the castle. I marveled again at the rubies, emeralds, sapphires, and diamonds that studded its surface. Bigger than eyeballs, any one of them would have been worth a fortune in the upper world.

We passed through tall wooden doors and into the long corridor that leads to the enormous Throne Room.

The last time I'd been in that room, it had been crowded with happy, boisterous goblins. Now it was nearly empty. On the throne, which rested atop a dais four steps high, sat the king. He looked gloomy, but at least he was in one piece. This was better than when his head had been in a wooden box and his body had been locked in the top of one of the towers.

When he saw us, King Nidrash stood and spread his arms. He was big for a goblin, an inch or two taller than me. "Welcome, Goblin Friends," he said. His voice was soft and subdued, and despite his smile I could hear sadness in it.

On the third step of the stone dais sat Borg, the elderly goblin who was the king's counselor. He, too, had risen when we came in, but had soon sat again.

Once we had introduced Bwoonhiwda and Werdolphus, the king said, "Again you come to us in time of need, Fauna."

I was surprised that he spoke directly to me rather than to one of the adults. But it made sense, in a way. Having a conversation with Igor was always difficult, and Bwoonhiwda and Werdolphus were newcomers. I was the one the king already knew.

I bowed, then said, "What is your need, King Nidrash?"

"A wizard named Helagon has been stirring up discontent among my goblins. The joy and energy of Nilbog are being drained away. It is worst among the young. The scamps have become rebellious, and many have run away. Goblin mothers are in despair."

"I do not know what we can do to change this."

He raised a hand. "Let me finish. Last night one of the scamps came back. He returned because he had become frightened of what Helagon is up to and had decided to let us know about it. This is why I have brought you here. I know you are seeking *the* William. But I am quite certain that our problem with Helagon and your problem with William and the stone toad are woven together."

"That's interesting," said a voice from beside me.

While everyone else was looking around, trying to see where the voice had come from, I cried, "William! You're back!"

"I thought it was time for another Sleep Walk."

The king blinked. "Where is he? I hear him but cannot see him!"

I explained about the Sleep Walk potion. The king seemed to find this perfectly sensible. When I was done, he closed one eye, then pressed a finger on either side of his other eye, causing it to bulge out in a disturbing way. "Ah, there you are!" he cried. "Most glad to see you, William. Can you tell us where your body is?"

William shook his head. "Somewhere in Nilbog, I'm certain. But *exactly* where, I couldn't say. We've moved around a lot. I get the feeling the toad is afraid of something. I can't explore unless I do a Sleep Walk, and as soon as I drank the potion, I came straight to Fauna to find out what's been happening."

At that moment another goblin came stumbling into the room. He was nearly as tall as the king, and quite skinny for a goblin. He had bare feet and wore a badly stained robe. As he got closer, I saw that the stains were from ink. His orange hands were speckled with ink too. I figured this must be John's friend Stanklo.

"I just got word of our visitors!" he burst out. "Are we going to take them to see her? You know I must be present if I am to record such events."

"See who?" I asked.

Borg heaved himself to his feet once more. Gasping a bit, he said, "We have a visitor who knows a great deal about the toad and where it came from. Shall I lead them to her, O my king?"

"Let's all go," Nidrash replied.

He led us behind the throne, where we entered a stone tunnel. Just inside the tunnel was a rack of glowing-fungus torches. Each of us with a body took one.

The passage sloped downward. It forked several times, which made it hard to keep track of our route. My stomach grew tight. The trip was bringing up memories of being in the goblin dungeon the year before, which was not an experience I wanted to repeat. I thought we could trust the king, but I wasn't entirely certain.

At last we entered a cave about the size of the one where we had met Wongo. On its far side was a rounded white wall. As we approached, a burst of light from behind the wall revealed that it was not white but made of clear crystal.

On the other side of the crystal wall stood a beautiful woman. She was dressed in a white robe and had long red hair that hung nearly to her waist. Something twitched at the back of my mind when I saw her, and I thought, *Why does she look so familiar?*

"It the book lady!" Igor shouted.

"What do you mean?" I asked.

"The book lady! The one who tell Igor to give book to William."

"Yes, that's Sophronia," Werdolphus confirmed.

The woman didn't seem disturbed at a voice coming from nowhere. Did this mean she could see him? Or was she just used to ghosts?

"Why are you behind that wall?" I asked.

"Who's that?" she asked. "Is the king with you?"

"I'm here," said the king. Turning to us, he explained, "She can't see us. The wall is clear only from this side."

Well, that explained why she hadn't been disturbed

by not seeing Werdolphus. She couldn't see any of us!

When the king told Sophronia who he had with him, she cried, "Thank goodness! There is much you need to know, and time is running out."

"Why are you behind that wall?" I asked again. "Are you a prisoner?"

"No, no. The goblins are protecting me, for which I owe them great thanks. A wizard named Helagon is after me. If he captures me, he will . . . Well, I might be persuaded to give him information he desperately desires but must not have. This chamber blocks my magic so that he cannot find me."

"What do you do foh food and dwink?" Bwoon-hiwda asked.

"Once a day the goblins bring them to me. We raise the crystal wall by a couple of inches, and they quickly slide them through. Then we seal it again. Now listen! There are things you need to know—things I would have told you at the Baron's castle had I not been prevented from reaching you. And there are things I need to know as well. Tell me quickly, please, what happened the night the toad came to life."

Since William and I were the only ones who had been there when it happened, it was up to us to tell the story. Sophronia's eyes grew wide as we spoke, but she let us tell everything—including what we had done since—without interrupting.

When I retold Bonecracker John's story about the giant and the wicked wizard, William exclaimed, "So *that's* where the toad came from! If I had known that, we wouldn't have messed around with it."

"I intended for you to 'mess around' with it," Sophronia replied. "It's why I brought the book. Only, I planned to be there with you when you used it."

"So where were you when we needed you?" I asked angrily.

Sophronia's eyes grew dark. "Someone betrayed me to my enemies, and I was being pursued. When I reached the castle, I left the book with Igor so that if I was caught, it would not be lost. Then I fled to draw the enemy away. I'd hoped to return the next night, but the pursuit was relentless. I managed to elude it long enough to find shelter here in Nilbog, many thanks to the king. Now listen! Time is pressing. Old John's story of Harry and the wizard is true as far as it goes. But, as with so many tales, there is another level, one that will completely change the way you view it. And you have a lot to do with it, William."

"How can I have anything to do with it? It happened before I was born!"

"Just listen! What John told your friends was the exact story my husband and I wanted people to believe. But there is a story *beneath* that story, a story about a game of power that has stretched across centuries. Now that game has reached its crisis point. The danger is rising, and if things go amiss, there will be fearsome consequences . . . beginning with the destruction of Nilbog."

"What?" I cried.

"Helagon does not want the stone simply as a plaything. He wants to open the Pit of Thogmoth. If he succeeds, all of Nilbog will be destroyed."

"Pit sound bad," Igor said. "What is it?"

It was Stanklo who answered. "Beneath Nilbog lies a terrifying place of fire and demons. With the help of several powerful human magicians, we sealed it shut over two hundred years ago. It was the finest human-goblin collaboration ever."

"Why would Hewagon want to open it?" Bwoon-hiwda asked.

"That's the great mystery," Sophronia replied. "Possibly for wealth. It is rumored that there is a trove of gold and jewels in Thogmoth. But mere wealth seems beneath Helagon. It might be to raise an army of demons to aid him in conquering the world. Perhaps it is just for the destructive joy of it."

"But doing that would be madness," the king objected.

"Helagon is mad, bad, and dangerous to know," Sophronia replied. "But then, no one really does know him. We know something drives him and he will stop at nothing to reach his goals. But *what* drives him, and what those goals are—money, power, or something darker and more dangerous—we cannot discern. Now listen. You need to know the rest of the story. John was correct when he told you it was rumored the wizard who was turned into the stone toad had sought the Black Stone of Borea. The stone had long been lost, but that had not stopped many a power-mad magic-maker from lusting for it. Helagon was the worst of them, and has made obtaining it his life's ambition."

"We found a warning about him carved into the pedestal that held the stone toad," I said.

"Yes, I put it there myself. Helagon was the one we were trying to shield the stone from at the time John has told you of."

"How could you have done that?" Werdolphus said. "You wouldn't even have been born at that time."

Sophronia flicked her hand, as if brushing his comment aside. "I've spent most of the last seventy-five years in a magical sleep that keeps me from aging. I wake but once a year, in order to check on the toad."

"Does Helagon do that too?" I asked.

Sophronia's mouth twisted. "I don't know how Helagon manages to stay young, and I would rather not think on it. His method is likely dark, disturbing, and cruel. Now let me continue. My husband and I are part of a group of wizards called the League of Teldrum. The League has worked for centuries to keep the stone away from those who would abuse its power. Now watch, and I will show you the *true* story of the stone toad!"

Stories are like onions. They have many layers, and can make you cry.

—Stanklo the Scribbler

CHAPTER SIXTEEN

THE STORY BENEATH THE STORY

Sophronia stepped back from the crystal wall and made a series of gestures. Images appeared on the wall's clear surface. To my surprise, the people in the images were *moving*. It was as if one of the paintings in the Baron's castle had come to life! Soon I realized that the pictures were acting out the story Sophronia was telling.

"At the time John told you of," she said, "the stone had been missing for many years. My husband—Edrick is his name—learned that it had somehow found its way into the village where the giant, Harry, lived."

A picture of the village appeared. People were walking in the streets. Then we saw Harry towering over the houses. No wonder his mistakes had caused such big problems!

"Though Edrick had discovered that the stone was in the village, he had no idea where."

"Shouldn't he have been able to sense something that powerful?" William asked.

Sophronia shook her head. "You would think that would be likely, if you didn't understand the stone. It is . . . well, it's almost as if the thing had a mind of its own and was trying not to be found. Our concern was that launching a full-scale search would alert Helagon. So we concocted a desperate plan. The giant, Harry, was part of it." Sophronia smiled for the first time since we had met her. "In truth, John's relative was a bit brighter than the official story gives him credit for."

The image of a handsome man appeared on the crystal wall.

"This is my husband, Edrick. After getting Harry to agree to help us, Edrick disguised himself as a minor but extremely greedy wizard."

The image showed Edrick twisting his spine and hunching over. His curly brown hair turned gray and scraggly. His eyes bulged and looked quite mad. Raising his hands, he clutched at the air. As he did, his fingers grew long and bony.

I gasped. This was the man I had seen in the mirror I found in the pedestal!

"It pained Edrick to assume this hideous form," Sophronia said. "And not just because he was a bit vain of his looks. The twisting of bone and the stretching of flesh required for such a transition is agonizing. However, it was necessary to shield him from the eyes of our enemies.

"Much of what happened next is just as John told you. Edrick, in his role of greedy wizard, demanded ever-increasing tribute from the townspeople, always hoping for the Black Stone to show up."

We watched as villagers lined up at the wizard's tower, carrying everything from chairs to chickens.

"I'm sure the people were thrilled with that," I said sourly. I was annoyed by the way Sophronia and her husband had treated these poor villagers.

"They were unhappy and furious," Sophronia replied sharply. "And they had every reason to be. But it was vital that Edrick not seem to be looking for the stone itself."

"Why?" William asked.

"Because it would alert Helagon to what we were after! The man had spies everywhere. Believe me, the townspeople would have been far more unhappy if Helagon had come sweeping in to find the stone. It's unlikely *his* search would have left a building standing!"

She took a breath, as if trying to calm herself, then said, "It wasn't until the villagers had brought almost everything they owned that Edrick found the stone among their offerings. This is why it had to be Edrick who did this, by the way. In all the League he was the only one powerful enough to resist the stone's ability to suck out a wizard's magic. Anyway, once he had the stone safely in hand, he delivered the final threat, the Spell of Stonely Toadification."

"If he already had what he wanted, why did he keep threatening the villagers?" I asked, more annoyed than ever.

Sophronia smiled. "Keep listening. The threat was the cue for young Will Smith, who was in on the plan, to fetch Harry. This is where your ancestor comes into the story, William."

The image on the crystal wall now showed a boy, who looked a great deal like my William, dashing out of the village. He arrived, panting, in front of a cave. Unlike in John's story, Harry wasn't shaving. But after Will told him something, he hung a mirror around his neck and then patted lather all over his face. That done, he picked up Will and started for town.

Sophronia spoke again. "When Edrick threw the blast of magic that struck Harry's mirror, it was not bad luck that sent it flying back toward Edrick. We had crafted Harry's mirror specifically to attract and reflect the magic . . . and Edrick was wearing an amulet designed to catch it. When the magic struck Edrick, he was holding the Black Stone. As he transformed, the stone was encased within his toadly form—and thus safely hidden from the world!"

The image on the crystal wall showed Edrick's "nasty wizard" form becoming the stone toad we knew so well.

Tears leaked from Sophronia's eyes. "The League and I had hoped to return my dear one to human shape in only a few years. But our enemies were constantly watching, and we dared not risk losing the stone. Finally I opted to take the magical sleep, waking but once a year to visit Toad-in-a-Cage Castle, where the stone toad had been taken for safekeeping."

"So that's why you kept showing up!" Werdolphus said.

"Of course!"

"Wait!" I said. "Did you need food and water while you slept?"

"No, the spell had protections to keep me safe from those needs. Why?"

I explained our concerns about the Baron. She bit her lip and shook her head. "This is bad. That spell clearly came from Helagon, and it is unlikely he bothered to protect the Baron. Bwoonhiwda was right—he must wake or perish."

"What can we do?" William cried.

"Defeat Helagon, which will not be easy. Now let me finish my story so you will understand. After many years another problem arose. We needed Will Smith to work the spell that would return Edrick to his true form."

"Why?" William asked.

"Because we had placed some of the magic that would be needed inside him."

"Why in the world did you do that?" I asked.

"It was another safeguard. Even if Helagon figured out where the stone was, he couldn't get at it without knowing about Will and getting him to cooperate. That cooperation was part of the spell. Will had to be *willing*! A bit of a pun, but an important one. Anyway, because of this I also checked on Will each year. Our young friend was not taking the magical sleep, so naturally he grew older. People sometimes fear age,

188

but I envied William. I longed to be with Edrick, living a normal life, growing old together, rather than being awake for only a few days every year." She sighed heavily, then said, "One year when I woke, I learned that Will had died unexpectedly. I grieved to lose our friend. I also cursed myself that we had been so cautious for all these years. But really, there had not been a time when we'd felt it was safe to return Edrick to his true self. Fortunately, Will had a son who would also work as part of the restoration spell, for the magic had been designed to pass to the next generation at his death. Alas, that son, also named Will, had gone missing!

"I was frantic. I would never get Edrick back if we couldn't find Will. I informed the League of the situation, and we began a desperate search. After many decades we located Will's great-great-grandson, and just in time! There was a war going on, and the boy, a mere infant, had been orphaned. He likely would have died had the League not found him. We delivered the baby to the Baron's castle, where he was raised in secret."

"Me?" William asked.

I was the only one who could see how wide his eyes were at this story.

"Of course you," Sophronia replied.

"But why in secret?" he asked.

"Because if nobody knew who you were, then nobody who might want to use you to wake the toad and release the stone would find you. We didn't even tell the Baron how important you were."

William was shaking his head, as if he couldn't believe what he was hearing.

Sophronia continued her story. "Now, each year when I visited the castle, I would check on both my husband and you, William. This year you were finally old enough to participate in the spell that would rouse Edrick from his long and stony sleep. I was filled with joy at the thought of seeing my beloved husband in his true form again. But I was too eager, and so let that eagerness overwhelm our years of caution. Though I was heartbroken and horrified when I had to flee, I didn't worry about Edrick, as I assumed he'd remain safe in the castle. It never occurred to me you would begin to break the spell on your own!"

"It does seem awfully convenient that William and Fauna managed that," Werdolphus said.

Sophronia shook her head. "There was nothing convenient about it! I'm not sure what happened to start things—it might even have been the book itself, wanting to be used after all these years." She sighed, and tears trembled in her eyes. "My poor, half-transformed Edrick. I don't know if he is even aware of his real identity. I suspect the reason he took you, William, was that he sensed you are somehow important to him. I can promise you he would never hurt you. But he has to be horribly confused, being trapped in that stone body." She turned to the rest of us and said, "You *must* find him before Helagon does. Find him and help him regain his true form."

"How are we supposed to do that?" I asked.

"You'll need the book and the mirror."

I groaned. "We left them at the castle."

"Why in the world did you do that?" Sophronia cried.

"How in the world were we supposed to know we should bring them?" I snapped, angry at the way she assumed we should have known to bring them with us. "It's not as though anyone told us."

"I'm sorry," Sophronia said. "That was uncalled-for on my part. It's just that I'm so desperate."

"Well, Karl figured it out, and he's bringing them. But we have no idea when he'll get here."

I decided it was kinder not to mention that I thought it was unlikely he would arrive at all. To be honest, I wasn't that worried about whether this Edrick got back to human form. But clearly we were going to have to deal with him to rescue William.

Sophronia twisted her hands. "Now that the awakening has begun, there is a time limit to complete it. If Edrick is not returned to human form by the next full moon, he will forever be trapped as a toad. You must release him. And Helagon must *not* get the stone!"

Stanklo cleared his throat. When we looked at the ink-stained goblin, he said, "The next full moon is tomorrow night."

Sophronia gasped.

"Speaking of time . . . ," said William. He took out his watch, flipped it open, then cried, "Yow! I have to get back to my body, and fast!"

Instantly he was gone.

Stanklo shook his head. "As I was about to say, under the circumstances, it might be best for these travelers to follow the plan suggested by Guardian Wongo and make their way to Flegmire's cave. Though she is quite mad, she often has uncanny insights. And she might know where the toad is hiding."

King Nidrash stroked his chin. Finally he said, "I agree, Stanklo. But they must have a guard."

"Likely to attract attention," Borg objected.

"Then instruct the group assigned to follow at a moderate distance and approach only if there is an attack. Also, we need someone to show our visitors the way."

"Herky know way to Flegmire's cave," Herky said softly. He was trembling, obviously terrified. "Herky do it for William."

As we left the underground city, we were followed by Captain Grickle and the Seventh Mischief, the same goblin guard group that had rescued us earlier. I didn't particularly like the idea of their trailing us. Even so, it was good to know we had backup if there were any problems. And they stayed far enough behind us that it was almost as if they weren't there.

We had been walking for two or three hours when we came to a downhill path so steep we spent the next several minutes doing nothing but watching our feet. When the path leveled out, I looked up and gasped at the towering pillars of white and tan ahead of us.

"What mushwooms!" Bwoonhiwda said.

I had to agree. The mushroom closest to me had a stem too big to put my arms around. Unlike a tree, its "trunk" was perfectly smooth. Even more interesting, from its gills—and from those of the mushrooms all around it—drifted thousands of glowing spores, like fireflies floating to the ground. The gills themselves also gave off a gentle glow. Together they made this part of the underground world bright as a cloudless night with a full moon.

"Does the light hurt your eyes?" I asked Sterngrim.

"It's not bad. It was the fiery glare of your torch that upset my people so much. *That* was too bright!"

We walked on in silence. Finally we stepped from between two giant mushrooms into a clear space.

Some thirty feet ahead of us was a wall of rock.

At the base of this underground cliff was a cave.

Coming from the cave was the most horrifying sound I had ever heard.

"Sounds wike someone is doing tewwible things to kitties," said Bwoonhiwda, who had stepped up beside me.

"Told you!" Herky whined. "Flegmire probably eating a little goblin right now!"

Everything in me wanted to turn and run. But Wongo and Stanklo had both said Flegmire was our best chance to find William. Since William was my friend and I was part of the reason he was in this mess, I figured I should be the one to do it.

"Stay here," I whispered. "I'll go talk to her."

"Absowutewy not!" Bwoonhiwda replied. "I go!"

"Igor go too" growled Igor. He raised his bear over his head and added, "Any trouble, Igor bop it! Igor protect Bwoonhiwda!"

"I don't need pwotection, you big wug!"

"Igor come anyway," he said stubbornly.

In the end we all went, with Bwoonhiwda and Igor in the lead.

When we reached the cave, we clustered at the edge and peered in.

I blinked, trying to figure out what in the world I was seeing.

In all of Nilbog there is no stranger goblin than Flegmire. Her sense of mischief is deep and subtle. Were she not completely mad she would have a place of high honor at court.

—Stanklo the Scribbler

CHAPTER SEVENTEEN

FLEGMIRE

In the center of Flegmire's cave, which was dimly lit by lamps filled with glowing fungus, stood a big frame. I thought it was made of wood until I realized that since no trees grow underground, it must have been made from giant mushrooms.

The frame was divided into square boxes about two feet on a side. Each row had three boxes, and the frame was four rows high, making twelve boxes in all.

Strapped inside each box except one was a small goblin.

A hideous female goblin—the oldest and ugliest I had ever seen—was pulling their tails! Each time she yanked a tail, the goblin it was attached to would squeal or shriek or scream. Sometimes the old goblin would give three quick tugs, sometimes a long one. Once she used both hands to pull two different tails, and at the same time kicked one of the goblins on the first level in the butt, so three squeals blended together. The sound was horrible, but the sight of those little goblins being tortured was even worse.

"This is not wight!" Bwoonhiwda shouted as she strode into the cave. "Wet those gobwins be, you wicked woman!"

The old goblin—Flegmire, I assumed—looked up. "Ah, there you are!" Her voice was low and gravelly, but she spoke as if nothing at all was wrong. "I was wondering when you would show up! All right, boys, that'll do for today. See you tomorrow, same time, same station."

To my surprise the little goblins unstrapped themselves and scrambled out of the frame. Laughing and shouting, they scampered past us and disappeared among the giant mushrooms.

"Why were you torturing them?" I demanded.

Flegmire looked puzzled. "Torturing? We were *practicing.*"

Bwoonhiwda pounded the butt of her spear on the floor. "Pwacticing what? Being mean to young gobwins?"

"Don't be absurd," said Flegmire, stroking the frame that had held the goblins. "This is the goblin harmonium. Invented it myself! You fill it with little goblins, and by pulling their tails, you make music. We're preparing a concert for the king!" Noticing Herky, she said, "Oooh! I need someone who squeals in B-flat. Think that little muffin could do it?"

Herky squealed, but I didn't think it was a B-flat.

"Do not mowest this gobwin!" said Bwoonhiwda, stepping in front of him.

Flegmire shrugged. "Doesn't have the sound I need anyway, drat the flumsies. All right, let's get down to cronkers. I know why you've come."

"How can you know that?" I asked.

She shrugged her bony shoulders. "Pretty much everything filters down to Flegmire sooner or later, my little kumquat. As I understand it, young William, hero of the goblins, is now captive of the giant stone toad that used to sit in a cage in that unspeakable castle where the spirit of every goblin except me was held prisoner for over a hundred years."

She shuddered, and her enormous eyes rolled around a bit. Then she said, "Let me tell you, those were a long hundred and twenty-one years. Sure, I wasn't captured. But I had no one to talk to for all that time. Can you wonder that I went a little bonkers?" Crossing her eyes, she hooked a finger over her lower lip and flicked it, making a *Buh-beep, buh-beep, buh-beep, buh-beep* sound.

I took a step back.

"Only fooling, dearie! I'm as sane as brixels in a fleempit!"

As I stepped forward again, Sterngrim whispered, "Remember what Wongo told you about how to talk to her!"

I nodded. Though it irked me to be polite to someone who had just been yanking the tails of little goblins, I said, "May I speak, O Wisest of the Wise?"

"Nice to see someone has remembered her manners! Yeah, go ahead and talk. Assuming you have something to say, of course. Don't waste my time with blather. Got enough of that in my head already." With that, she smacked herself in the back of the head and cried, "Shut up in there!"

She closed her eyes for a minute, then smiled. "All right, the voices are quiet. You can talk now."

Baffled, and a little scared, I said, "The troll guarding the entrance to Nilbog said you would roll the bones for us."

"Oh, he did, did he? That Wongo is a fine one for

making promises with other people's time. Probably said I should let you look in my Vision Pool, too?"

"He didn't mention it."

"Dang! Should have kept my big gob shut. Oh, well. Since I brought it up, I'll probably have to show you. The question now is which to do first, roll the bones or show the pool, show the pool or roll the bones. Ah! I know! I'll roll the bones to decide! Of course, first you have to pay the price."

"Price?" I asked.

"Pwice?" Bwoonhiwda echoed.

"Yeah, price. If I'm gonna tell you the secrets of the present and the future, I need to have a bit of the past to make up for it. Kind of balances things out. Otherwise the world might explode in burbles. So I need a secret. And it better be a doozy, or you ain't gettin' nothin'."

I felt my insides freeze. I had kept my secret for more years than I could count. I couldn't tell it now. I couldn't.

But what if I had to?

For a while no one said anything. Then Herky stepped forward.

Relief surged through me. I would be willing to overlook a lot of future naughtiness for this.

Looking directly at Flegmire, he said, "Once, Herky swiped his brother's lizard sandwich."

Flegmire rolled her enormous eyes. "Not good enough. I could have guessed that anyway."

My heart sank. After a few more moments of silence, Bwoonhiwda stepped forward. She thumped her spear on the floor and said, "Sometimes I am afwaid!"

I held my breath, hoping Flegmire would accept this.

The old goblin nodded and stroked her chin. "Not bad, not bad at all." She tipped her head as if thinking, then said, "Not bad, but the bubbles in my brain say not good enough. Probably just as well. We can forget the whole thing and—"

"Wait!" cried Werdolphus.

Flegmire looked up. "You gonna tell me something, ghostie boy?"

By which it was clear that she could see him.

Werdolphus took a deep breath. Well, his chest expanded as if he was taking a deep breath. I don't know if ghosts actually breathe. Floating toward her, he said, "How about if I tell you how I died?"

Flegmire's eyes lit up. "Sounds interesting enough to choke a bleezer. But are you sure it's a secret?"

I stepped forward. "Pardon me, Wisest of the Wise, but it must be. I asked him how he died once, and he got so mad he just disappeared."

Flegmire nodded in satisfaction.

Werdolphus puffed out his chest and began a long story about a heroic battle in which he sacrificed his life to save a wounded friend. It was very exciting, but something about it bothered me. Finally I realized the problem. Though he had been killed by a cannonball, I also had the sense that he had died *inside* the castle.

I don't know how, but it was clear that Flegmire realized he was making it up. With a shriek she spit on the floor and cried, "That's a lie. Lies don't count! Out of here, all of you!"

To my surprise, the ghost looked as horrified as I felt. "Wait!" he cried, holding up his hands as if to stop Flegmire from throwing out the body he no longer had. "I'm sorry! It's just . . . well, that's the story I made up to tell myself after it happened. I've told it so many times, I guess it started to seem real. It's certainly the way I wish it had happened. I'll give you the real story this time, I promise!"

Flegmire made a face, then stuck a finger into her ear and closed her eyes. After a moment she nodded and pulled the finger out. Holding it in front of her, she said, "Mr. Pointer says you can have another chance. But you'd better tell the truth this time, or Mr. Pointer is going to have a very nasty surprise for you!"

His pale face serious, Werdolphus nodded toward the finger and said, "Thank you, Mr. Pointer."

"Well, let's hear it," said Flegmire. Then she stuck her finger back into her ear. I guess she was planning to listen to Werdolphus with her other ear.

The ghost looked around nervously. "Do *they* have to hear?" he asked.

"Yes indeedelee doo. Ain't gonna be a secret no more, so you might as well let 'em in on it right now."

Werdolphus straightened his shoulders, swallowed, then said, "I met my death as the result of a tragic cleaning accident."

Flegmire snorted.

"It's not funny!" Werdolphus shouted.

"No, no, it's not. I was just laughing at something Mr. Pointer said. Your story is very sad. Only, it's not a story yet. Let's hear some details."

Werdolphus sighed. "Forty years ago I went to work in Toad-in-a-Cage Castle. While I was there, I met a beautiful young woman named Hulda."

My eyes widened at this.

"Hulda was very serious, so I used to try to make her laugh. One of my jobs was to dust the cannonballs the Baron keeps on the mantel of the Great Hall's fireplace. The mantel is high, so I had to use a stepladder. Even with that I had to reach up to do the job. One day I was working away at this when I heard Hulda come into the room. I turned to make a face at her, and . . ."

His voice trailed off.

"Go on!" Flegmire demanded.

"I lost my balance. My left hand was behind one of the cannonballs. As I fell, I pulled the cannonball with me. When I hit the floor, the cannonball landed on my head. Killed me on the spot. I've been haunting the castle ever since."

I glanced at Bwoonhiwda and saw her lift her right braid. She stared at the cannonball woven into the bottom of it, then shuddered.

As for Flegmire, she let out a hoot of laughter. "Oh, that's a dilly. Definitely worth the price of admission. All right, let's roll the bones!"

She squatted on the floor, which made her knees considerably higher than her ears. Suddenly her eyes grew wide and she cried, "Whoa! Better step back!"

As we moved away, Flegmire farted with such vio-
lence that it lifted her nearly a foot off the floor.

We began to cough and choke at the horrifying
odor.

"Oh, stop fussing. The smell ain't gonna hurt you.
At least, not much. You might lose a little skin, but it'll
grow back. Now, where was I? Oh, right, the bones!"
She looked around. "Where in frootition did I put that
box? Ah, it's over there. You! Little goblin who can't
squeal a B-flat! Run over and fetch it for me."

Herky started for the box. I saw Bwoonhiwda pre-
pare to spring into action if Flegmire did anything to
threaten him.

Circling the ancient goblin, never taking his eyes
off her, Herky went to where she had pointed. The
box, which rested on a large boulder, was carved with
screaming faces.

Trembling, Herky carried it to Flegmire. When he
reached her, he placed it on the floor in front of her.

"See," she said sweetly, "I'm not so horrible."

Herky nodded and turned to go back to Bwoonhiwda. As soon as she had a shot at his rear end, Flegmire reached out and yanked his tail. He squealed,
clutched his bottom, and bolted away.

Flegmire shook her head sadly. "Thought with a

surprise he might do a B-flat after all. Ah, well. Guess the grimpets are in the sauce today."

With that, she lifted the lid of the box. It was hinged, so the raised lid blocked our view. Staring down, she muttered, "Oh, what lovely bones!"

Then she scooped out a handful of human knuckle-bones.

I would rather not explain how I knew what they were.

She cupped one of her long-fingered, knobby-knuckled hands over the other, shook the bones, then tossed them to the floor. Leaning over, she examined them, muttering, "What do I spy with my sweet little eye?"

It was an odd thing to say, since her eyes were the size of apples. They were also somewhat terrifying, especially when they pointed in different directions.

"What's she doing?" whispered a voice from beside me.

"William!" I cried.

"Be quiet!" Flegmire shrieked.

"Wow, she's cranky," William whispered. "We'd better not talk until she's done."

The others looked at me oddly. I gestured to indicate that William had rejoined us.

Flegmire twice stopped to look at a bone more closely. The second time, she picked it up, licked it, made an expression of disgust, then threw it over her shoulder. She continued to study the remaining bones until her wrinkled face broadened in a wide grin and she said, "There it is, plain as the warts on a binksniffer! We start with the pool." Leaping to her feet, she said, "Follow me!"

"We don't need to," I said. "William is here."

Flegmire looked at me, squinted a bit, then laughed. "Well, he's *part* here. Hello there, almost-invisible boy. Didn't really think you could fool *these* old eyes, did you?"

She put her fingers on her upper and lower eyelids and pulled them apart so that her already enormous eyes were bigger than ever.

"William really here?" Igor asked.

"Yes, I'm here, Igor."

"Can you lead us to your body now?" I asked.

"I think so. I didn't pass through any stone this time, so we should have a clear path back."

"Then wet's get moving!" Bwoonhiwda said.

"Not so fast, missy," Flegmire replied.

The idea of anyone calling Bwoonhiwda "missy" would have made me laugh if things hadn't been so tense just then.

I stepped forward. "Why should we wait, O Wisest of the Wise?"

Flegmire answered as if speaking to someone she thought was not very bright. "Because we have to look into the pool, duck fluff! The bones said so. Doesn't make any difference if you've found what you *think* you were looking for. Ignoring the bones is a good way to end up nothing but bones yourself. Any gloink can bunkle that one! Follow me if you know what's good for you!"

She turned toward the rear of the cave, then turned back and said, "Ooopsie! Almost forgot. This is gonna take another secret. And it better be a humdinger."

Coldness seized my heart.

Flegmire looked straight at me, and her next words moved me to flat-out terror. "I think it's your turn, my little pazoozle. What secret are *you* hiding?"

Secrets are like farts. The longer you hold one in, the more explosive it is when you finally let it go.

—Stanklo the Scribbler

CHAPTER EIGHTEEN

THE PRICE FOR THE POOL

"What makes you think I have a secret?" I asked, trying to mask my fear.

"Oh, everyone has a secret, dearie, even me. Of course, in my case I can't remember it, which sort of puts the frost on my bunkie. But I'm not the one seeking information, am I?"

I swallowed, then put my hand on Solomon's Collar and said, "I'm not supposed to be wearing this."

I heard a little cry of surprise from William.

Flegmire just snorted. "Not much of a secret. Knew it wasn't meant for you the moment I saw you."

"How could you know that?"

"Huh. Maybe *that's* my secret! Knew it was something.

Now come on, my little pickle. We both know you're hiding something bigger. Let's have it."

I was aware of the others looking at me, and I knew they wanted to ask about the collar. I was spared from answering that when Flegmire screamed, "Tick tock, time's up! Now go on, all of you. I have important things to do." Then she muttered, "Just hope I can remember what they are!"

"Wait! I'll tell you."

Flegmire smiled and settled back on her haunches. "Well, now we're getting somedingle. Come on, girl. Spill it."

I closed my eyes and whispered, "I don't know how old I am."

"Speak up, girl. I think I've got a potato in my ear."

Angry now, I shouted, *"I don't know how old I am!"*

Flegmire nodded but didn't say anything. I could tell she was waiting for more.

I glanced around. The others were looking at me oddly.

"Do you mean you don't know when your birthday is?" Werdolphus asked.

I could tell he was trying to be helpful, and I appreciated it. But I had to shake my head.

Flegmire cackled and rubbed her hands together.

"Now this is getting interesting. If it's not about your birthday, what is it about?"

"I told you—I don't know how old I am."

"Yeah, yeah, you said that. Still, not hard to guess. Humans age in a pretty standard way. You're about ten or eleven."

That pushed me over the edge. "Well, I've looked exactly the same way for at least seventy years now! Maybe longer. I have no idea! I told you, I don't know how old I am. I just stay this way, and stay this way, and stay this way. AND I HATE IT!"

I was trying not to cry, but my weird condition had made it impossible to ever get close to people. I had already gotten friendlier with William and everyone else in the castle than I should have. In another year, two at the most, they would start to wonder about me. Another year after that, they would be certain there was something strange.

After the first two times I'd been accused of witchcraft and barely escaped with my life, I understood that I must never stay in one place long enough to let people figure out my secret. And now I had blurted it out to this crazy old goblin—and everyone else in our group—just to figure out how to help William.

Igor stumped over to me. "Igor never know how

old he is either," he said, putting a thick hand on my shoulder.

I knew he meant it to be kind, but the idea that Igor and I were alike did not do much to make me feel better.

Flegmire bounced to her feet. "Now, *that* was a secret! Come on, you lot. We have to look into the pool before it's too late."

I was relieved there was no time to talk about what I had just told them. Still, Flegmire's words made me nervous. "Too late for what?"

The old goblin rolled her enormous eyes. "How should I know? Do you think the clocks talk to me? Well, they do, but all they say is 'Tick tock Bongaroo! Tick tock Bongaroo!' Be enough to drive me crazy if I wasn't already!"

She started for the back of the cave, where two sticks of wood—or mushroom, I suppose—seemed to rise directly out of the floor. As we got closer, I realized they actually came up through a hole. Even closer, and I saw that they were the top of a ladder.

We followed Flegmire down to another cave, much smaller and darker. It was moist and cool, and the air was surprisingly pleasant, filled with the clean smell that comes after a good rain.

What little light shone in this cave came from a glowing pool in its center. The pool was about five feet across, a perfect circle surrounded by a raised wall of stone about three feet high. That would have made it seem more like a well than a pool, if not for the fact that the water came all the way up to the edge of it.

Flegmire thrust her right arm into the water and began to stir. Soon the surface started to bubble.

"Yow!" she cried, yanking out her arm.

"What's wrong?" I asked.

"Nothin'. Just gets hot. That's how I know it's ready. Now, what do you want to see?"

"How would a nice librarian do for starters?" called a voice from behind us.

I spun and saw Karl standing on the ladder. He was clutching the book in one hand, and I could see the mirror strapped to his back.

"You came!" I cried.

"You needn't look so surprised." He sounded a little hurt.

"But how did you do it? Werdolphus said you had set out to find us, but I was afraid you would never make it."

"I might not have, if Werdolphus hadn't told me you were heading for Bonecracker John. I found a map that led me to him."

"Hah!" Igor bellowed. "Told Karl old Bonecracker was real!"

"Wet the man tawk!" Bwoonhiwda scolded.

"It's all right, Bwoonhiwda," Karl said. "I had that coming. Anyway, once I reached the giant's cave, he told me where you had gone and how to follow you."

"But what did you do for light?" I asked. "And how did you get past the lindlings?"

"The light came from the mirror," Karl replied. "It started to glow as soon as I entered the passage to Nilbog. As to lindlings . . . I don't even know what you're talking about!"

As I explained about winged lindlings, Sterngrim leaned close to my ear and said, "If the mirror was glowing too brightly, my fellow lindlings probably hid from the light."

Karl continued his story. "When I reached Wongo's cave, I found two goblins waiting to escort me to Nilbog. John had summoned them, via that grapevine thing of his. When we got to Nilbog, I found two more goblins waiting for me. The king had ordered them to bring me straight to you."

I had wondered how Karl could have caught up with us so quickly, but when I retraced our journey in my mind, I realized we had wasted a huge amount of time trailing the toad that first night and had gone well out of our way doing so. Coming directly would have been much faster.

"Burble, burble, burble!" shouted Flegmire. "You mizgorps wanna see what's in the pool or not? You gotta ask a question if you do. But better hurry. This won't last much longer."

"Show us what we need to do," I said at once.

"Boy, that's a tough order. Why don't you just ask to see the secret of true love?"

I didn't believe in true love, so that was not of interest to me.

"Can we hurry?" William cried. "I'm a little pressed for time. Remember, I can't stay out of my body for more than two hours."

Flegmire snorted. "Well, that's as fascinating as a clock in the pancake batter. Oooh! I've got something. Better come take a look. "

We hurried to the pool.

The picture in its water was as clear as the paintings in the Baron's castle. In the center was William's body, still and unmoving. It was surrounded by a reddish glow.

"What's that?" he asked, pointing to the glow.

"Got no idea," Flegmire said. "Never saw nothin'

like it, except for that time I made the mushroom wine too strong."

"I've got to go," William said urgently. Then he vanished.

There was no way to call him back, nothing to say, so I returned my attention to the image in the pool.

Close to William's body sat the stone toad. On some rocks about fifteen feet above them stood a tall, handsome man dressed in wizard's robes. I figured this must be Helagon.

"Where is the stone?" he demanded.

The voice startled me. I hadn't expected to be able to *hear* this. Flegmire's spell was even stronger than the one Sophronia had used back in Castle Nilbog.

I tried to figure out where the light came from, then realized the scene was at the edge of the mushroom forest. Was it possible they were not far away?

Helagon's demand for a reply went unanswered. The toad simply stared at him, blinking its big golden eyes. Scowling, the wizard raised his hands, moved them in a series of complicated gestures, then muttered a few words. Even though I couldn't make them out, they made me shiver. Then he shouted three words I did understand: "Speech be thine!"

Blue light flew from his hands. It struck the toad

on the nose, crackled around its body, then faded, as if sinking right into the toad.

The thing blinked its enormous eyes twice, then said in a deep, pleasant voice, "I do not have the stone."

"Nonsense! You've been shielding it ever since you and that dratted giant tricked me all those years ago."

"True. However, I did not bring it with me when I fled the castle."

"Why in the world not?" asked Helagon. He was calmer now, which made him seem even more dangerous.

"Because the spell was not completed, I did not know where I was, or even *what* I was. Memory has been returning, but slowly."

"If you were so confused, why bring the boy?"

"Something in me recognized him as key to my return to human form," the toad replied calmly.

At that moment two things happened. The image in the pool faded, and William returned.

From the look on his face I knew something terrible had happened.

"What is it?" I cried.

"I can't get back in!"

"What do you mean?"

"I can't get into my body! That wizard has blocked

it somehow. But if I don't get back in before the two hours are up, I'll be out of my body forever!"

"Oooh, that's bad," said Flegmire. "You'll end up like ghostie boy over there, except he has a chance of moving on if he ever learns to let go of the world. In your case, you'll have to stay a wandering spirit forever. Poor little guy. Just thinking of it makes me want to eat my toes in horror."

"Do you know anything that can help?" I cried.

"Mebbe."

"Well, what?"

Tugging her chin, Flegmire said, "Not sure I can remember. That kind of stuff used to be at the top of my bean, dearie. Sadly, when you're as old as I am, sometimes you have to glinkle the frizzit to bring back a thought. And that only works about half the time. Oh, I've got an idea! Throw a bucket of water on him—the actual body, I mean, not the see-through, floaty part."

"Water?"

Flegmire's eyes lit up, and she rubbed her bony hands together. "It'll crackle and fizzle and raise all sorts of jubapalooza. But it might to do the trick."

"But that's so simple."

"Lots of the complicated parts of magic are just for

show. There's a bucket in the upper cave you can borrow. But bring it back, or I'll set a gretchwangle on your trail."

"What's a gretchwangle?" Karl asked.

"Haven't figured that out yet, but when I do it will be plenty nasty. Be easier on both of us if you just bring back the bucket!"

"Thank you, O Wisest of the Wise," I said. "Ummm . . . could you tell from the image in the pool where Helagon and the toad are?"

Flegmire had started playing with her fingers and seemed to be ignoring the question.

"Flegmire!"

"Yeah, yeah, I heard you. I was trying to remember where it is. Finger games help me think." She looked up. Scratching an armpit, she said, "Ah, got it! Go out of my cave and turn right. Then walk on, sticking close to the cliffs until you get to the Big Face—"

"What's the Big Face?"

"Don't interrupt! You think it's easy for me to tell you this with gloops dancing in my beezlim? Now, where was I?" She stared into space for a minute, her eyes rolling around, then said, "Right . . . the Big Face. You'll know it when you see it. Stream flows out of its mouth. Lot of green moss in its nose, sort of like giant boogers. Cute, in a disgusting way. That's where you'll find them. About a thirty-minute walk from here."

William looked at his watch. "I only have forty-five minutes left!"

"Well, what are you waiting for?" Flegmire shouted. "Get moving!"

Sterngrim fluttering ahead of us, we scurried up the ladder and out of Flegmire's cave, making sure to grab the bucket as we went.

We were off to rescue William.

At least, that was what I thought.

I had no idea what was really in store for me.

When going to attack a wizard, it is vital to have a plan. It is also vital to remember that plans often go awry when magic enters the picture!

—*Stanklo the Scribbler*

CHAPTER NINETEEN

FACE-OFF AT THE BIG FACE

When we left the cave, we found Captain Grickle waiting for us.

"What do you want?" I said. I sounded rude, but I was feeling wildly impatient.

"Just to know where you are going. We will stay behind you, as ordered. But we must not lose you."

"We'll be following the line of the cliff," I said quickly. "You should be able to see us from the edge of the mushroom forest. You can track us that way."

Grickle stuck his finger into his nose and nodded, then bounded back to the Seventh Mischief.

"We have to get moving," William said urgently.

"We need to do some planning," Karl replied.

"Plan while we walk!" I said, and started out.

Karl hurried to stay up with me. "Fauna, we can't just march up to William's body with Helagon there. The wizard is extremely dangerous."

I knew Karl was right about doing some planning before we faced Helagon, but I couldn't stand any more delays. All I could think about was William, and whether he would be locked out of his body. Turning to Karl, I said, "You haven't explained what we have to do to return Edrick to human form. You did figure it out, right?"

"Yes. It takes the mirror, the book, the toad, and William." Looking toward where he had last heard William's voice, he said, "You'll be pleased to know that we have to get you back into your body before we do anything else. The spell requires you and the toad to look into the mirror in such a way that you see each other's eyes."

"Do you think we'll be able to get the toad to do that?" I asked.

Karl said, "From the way Edrick spoke to Helagon, I'm guessing he'll understand what we're trying to do. So we don't need to worry about that. The real problem is going to be disrupting the magic Helagon used to lock William out of his body. We'll need to distract him to do that. It really is a good thing he doesn't have the Black Stone."

"I wonder what happened to it," Werdolphus said. "After a hundred years it's amazing it's been lost again."

"Won't stay wost wong," boomed Bwoonhiwda. "Powah wike that attwacts wizahds wike cheese attwacts wats."

I shuddered at the thought of what might happen if some other magician found the Black Stone. Of course, a magic-user who didn't know how to handle the stone would just have the magic sucked right out of him, leaving nothing but an empty husk.

The thought made me glad I was not a magician.

"So we have to figure out how to distract Helagon," William said.

"Igor bop him!" cried Igor.

I shook my head. "Helagon would blast you with magic before you got within twenty feet of him."

Igor stamped around in a circle, shaking his bear.

I took this to mean he agreed with me and it made him mad.

Sterngrim nipped my ear. "What are they talking about?"

When I explained, she said, "What if I fly up from

behind, land on the back of his head, then have some fun with my claws and fangs? That ought to distract him!"

I translated this for the others. They agreed it was a good idea.

"Maybe you should ask that critter of yours to fly ahead right now and scout things out," William suggested. "I'd go myself, but last time I got a creepy feeling that Helagon could sense me. I'm afraid if I go back, it might put him on the alert."

I explained to Sterngrim what William had suggested.

"Good idea!" she said. She leaped from my shoulder and shot ahead. Soon she was out of sight.

The rest of us continued on foot. Well, except for William and Werdolphus, who floated. Drifting close to me, William said, "I'm so frightened, Fauna. If I was in my skin right now, I think I'd be throwing up."

A few minutes later Sterngrim landed on my shoulder and said, "Things haven't changed much from what we saw in Flegmire's pool."

"But how close are we?"

"Not far. Soon you'll find an inward curve in the cliff. It will be a good place to hide until I land on Helagon's head."

I explained to the others what Sterngrim had said. We decided that as soon as she attacked Helagon, Igor and Bwoonhiwda would charge in and scramble up the rocks to try to subdue him.

"Herky go too!" cried Herky eagerly. "Not big but can bite and bother! Herky good little fighty bad goblin!"

While Igor, Bwoonhiwda, and Herky attacked Helagon, I would fill the bucket with water to fling over William's body. William himself would hover close by so he could instantly plunge back into his skin if our plan worked.

Karl's job was to stay nearby with the book and the mirror so if we got William back into his body, we could return Edrick to his human form as quickly as possible. We would definitely need his help to deal with Helagon!

"What about me?" Werdolphus asked. "I'd like to help!"

"If you can think of anything you can do, feel free," I said.

The ghost sighed unhappily but obviously didn't have any ideas.

As we picked our way along by the eerie light of the mushroom forest, my fear grew. We had no idea how powerful Helagon truly was. For all I knew, ten minutes from now he would blast us to cinders. I wondered if he was so powerful he could even destroy a ghost, like Werdolphus, or a disembodied human, like William.

"Stop!" said Sterngrim suddenly. "Almost to the hiding place. You must move carefully to enter it without being seen."

Pressing tight to the cliffside, we proceeded as silently as possible.

When we reached the spot Sterngrim had in mind, I signaled the others to halt. Then I dropped to my belly and crawled forward to peer around the base of the cliff.

It was easy to see why the place was called the Big Face. The cliff jutted out in a way that looked like a man's profile. The face's enormous "nose" had a flat top about fifteen feet above the ground. On this spot, which was almost the size of a table, stood Helagon.

As Flegmire had described, a stream flowed from the base of the cliff, out of the place that would have been the mouth. William's body, still surrounded by that red glow, lay about fifteen feet downstream. Edrick-the-Toad crouched protectively beside it.

A moan from overhead made me look up. Spirit-William floated a few inches above me, also peeking around the outcropping.

I slid back to tell the others what we had seen.

"No point in waiting," Karl said.

I agreed. "Sterngrim, fly around so you can land on Helagon's head. Werdolphus, maybe you *can* help. Not counting when you are heading back to the castle, how far can you get from the cannonball?"

He thought for a moment, then said, "I could go anywhere in the castle."

Given the size of the castle, that gave him a fair range. "Good. Circle behind Helagon with Sterngrim. As soon as she's in place, get back here and let us know. That way Bwoonhiwda, Igor, and Herky can start out the instant Sterngrim attacks and we won't lose a second."

"We should get in fwont of you," Bwoonhiwda said.

I stepped back so the three could move into place.

Sterngrim flapped into the air, Werdolphus floating behind her.

"Seven minutes left," said William, staring at his watch.

I wanted to tell him not to worry, to reassure him that everything would turn out fine. But if I said that, the collar would start to choke me.

Two minutes later—William was timing it—Werdolphus returned and said, "Go!"

Igor, Bwoonhiwda, and Herky shot around the

cliff. The rest of us followed close behind. We made almost no sound, and Helagon didn't notice us until we were within a few feet of the stream. He raised his hands to shoot a blast of magic at us, then bellowed in pain as Sterngrim landed on his head and sank her claws into his flesh. When she wrapped her snaky body around his face and flapped her wings against his eyes, he screamed in rage.

I raced for the stream. It was too shallow at the edge to fill the bucket, so I waded into the center. As I dipped the bucket into the water, Helagon cried, "Scamps, attack!"

As the words left his lips, a group of goblins with red headbands came screaming around the other side of the Big Face.

I thought it was over for us then. But just as the first of the headband goblins leaped up to grab Igor by the heels, Captain Grickle and the Seventh Mischief and Marching Society came racing out of the mushroom forest.

With cries of "For king and Nilbog!" they hurtled toward the red headbands. Soon pairs of goblins were grappling and wrestling all over the area around the Big Face.

Igor, Bwoonhiwda, and Herky continued their

climb toward Helagon. I lifted the bucket and started toward William's body. As I did, I heard another cry from Helagon.

His voice held no rage now. This time it was a cry of pure triumph. The sound chilled my blood.

I looked up. Sterngrim was nowhere in sight. What had he done to her?

"You see what a waste this was, Edrick?" Helagon said. "Your friends have actually brought the Black Stone straight to me!"

Brought him the stone? What was he talking about?

Helagon made a gesture. The cannonball bound into the end of Bwoonhiwda's left braid floated into the air, lifting the braid with it. Bwoonhiwda cried out in rage. She grabbed the braid and pulled on it.

Her efforts had no effect. The braid continued to rise.

Edrick moaned in despair.

The end of the braid floated slowly toward Helagon's hand. When the braid was stretched to its full length, it pulled Bwoonhiwda off the rocks and into the air.

"Wet me down!" she bellowed. *"Wet me down!"*

At the same time, Igor leaped from the rocks. He had his bear in one hand, of course. But as he fell, he used his free hand to grab the other braid, the one *not* rising toward Helagon. He landed in a crouch about five feet from the base of the cliff, dropped his bear, and with both hands took a firm grip on Bwoonhiwda's right braid.

The left braid, the one being summoned by Helagon, continued its slow rise. Clearly what we had once believed to be a simple cannonball was actually the Black Stone of Borea. How had it ended up in Bwoonhiwda's braid? There was no time to think about that now. Soon the two braids formed a straight line that stretched from where Igor clutched the bottom of the right braid almost all the way to where Helagon stood. *Almost* all the way, but not quite. The Black Stone quivered about three feet below his grasp, and he couldn't reach down for it without toppling off the rocks.

In the middle of that straight line, nearly ten feet above the ground, was Bwoonhiwda.

"Hewagon, wet me woose, or I am going to thwash you and thwottle you!"

In response the wizard twisted the hand summoning the Black Stone. The stone began to turn, causing Bwoonhiwda to rotate in midair.

All around us goblin fought goblin. Their shrieks, shouts, and moans filled the air.

"Fauna!" cried William. "I'm down to my last minute!"

I started forward again, then stumbled over a rock.

William screamed in frustration.

Struggling to keep the bucket from tipping, I hit the water face-first, my hands extended in front of me. I felt the bucket being pulled from my grip. Lifting my head, I saw that Karl had it.

Spirit-William hovered close by, his face a mask of hope and terror.

Karl raced between two pairs of wrestling goblins and poured the water over William's body. A blaze of multicolored sparks, jewel-bright, erupted around his chest. With them came a hissing-crackling sound that was almost deafening.

Crying out in joy, Spirit-William plunged toward Flesh-William.

He bounced right off his own body.

"It didn't work!" he wailed. "We did it in time, but Flegmire was wrong! Now the time is up and I'm locked out forever."

When all is said and done, what's been done is more important than what's been said.

—*Stanklo the Scribbler*

CHAPTER TWENTY

IF I GAVE YOU

The despair in William's voice wrung my heart.

Then I heard another cry. It was Herky. Turning toward the Big Face, I saw the little goblin scramble up Igor's back. He leaped from Igor's shoulder to Bwoonhiwda's braid, climbed the braid, crawled over her head, and shinnied up the other braid to the Black Stone, which still quivered inches from Helagon's beckoning hand.

Herky then leaped from the stone to Helagon himself.

Grabbing the wizard around the waist, he squeaked, "Helagon bad! Herky bad sometimes, but Helagon bad all the time! Your momma should be ashamed, you bad Helagon!"

Then he sprang sideways, grabbed the arm the wizard was using to summon the Black Stone, and swung on it.

The sudden weight pulled Helagon's arm down. In that moment his magical grip was broken.

The stone plummeted down.

So did Bwoonhiwda's braid.

So did Bwoonhiwda.

"Igor catch you!" cried Igor, extending his arms and running in a circle.

Bwoonhiwda crashed into him, and they fell to the ground.

Helagon moved his hands again, muttering something that made no sense to me until I saw the result. The end of Bwoonhiwda's braid was unraveling! Soon it would release the Black Stone so he could get it after all.

I splashed out of the stream. As the last strands of the braid came undone, I flung myself over the stone. I was terrified. Would the stone begin to rise again, carrying me with it? Or would it just pull the life force right out of me?

Neither of those things happened. Instead, I remained on the ground, the stone clutched under my belly.

A tingle around my neck explained the reason. Solomon's Collar was working—somehow countering Helagon's magic!

Suddenly the cries of the battling goblins vanished. In the silence I looked up and saw a clear blue dome, like an upside-down bowl. It covered Helagon and me. The battling goblins had been pushed aside, but my friends were within it. All except Herky. Like Sterngrim, he had disappeared. What had Helagon done with him?

The wizard gazed down at me. "Now, this is interesting," he said. His voice was smooth and silky, a perfect match for his handsome face. "Obviously you have something that is blocking my magic, child. What is it?"

"Leave the girl alone!" Edrick bellowed.

"Speech be gone!" Helagon snarled. A bolt of red energy flew from his hands and rippled around Edrick. The toad opened his mouth, but no sound came out. His great golden eyes bulged with rage.

I wanted to stand up and spit in Helagon's face, but he was fifteen feet above me. Besides, I knew I had to continue protecting the stone. So I stayed huddled over it, refusing to look up, terrified of what would happen if he could catch my eye.

"You know," he said gently, "we could make a bargain."

I wanted to cover my ears to shut out his voice. It was filled with a tender care that I knew was false but that was almost impossible to resist. Only, I didn't dare move. I had to stay as I was, blocking the stone from him.

The wizard's next words struck new terror into me.

"Ah, your name is Fauna. Is that right?"

Was he reading my mind? If so, then let him read the way I felt about him! That should curl his perfect hair.

I guess he was immune to my anger, since his hair stayed straight. Then I remembered he had had his goblins search my cottage. So maybe he already knew my name.

"Why did you send those goblins to search my home?" I asked.

"Because I thought you might have the Black Stone."

"Why in the world would you think that?"

He did not answer directly. Instead he said, "Do you understand what I can do with that stone, Fauna? It's not just ruling the world, though that is a lovely thought. No, what I'm talking about is the fact that with the power at my control I will be able to do favors . . . pleasant things . . . for those who helped me when I needed it. You could be one of those friends, Fauna. You could be one of my favorites."

The warmth in his voice grew deeper, as if he were caressing me with words. "With the power of this stone, I will even be able to read the past. So let me ask you, dear Fauna. How would you like to know where you came from, and why you don't age?"

He *was* reading my mind! Fury raged through me, but also desire for what he was offering.

"I can answer those things for you, if I have the stone."

Do not listen to him! cried my brain. *No good can come of this!*

But my heart, my hungry and traitorous heart, was crying, *Yes! Yes, I want to know! I* need *to know!*

And that was true. I did need to know these things. For the first time since I had captured the stone, I looked up at him.

"Fauna!" said William, who was floating beside me.

"Be quiet!" I snapped.

I saw the others around me, Karl and Bwoonhiwda and Igor. Even Werdolphus, floating bodiless beside the bodiless William. They were all watching me, their faces twisted in a strange mix of hope and fear.

Hope and fear, but no answers. No answers for the questions that had bedeviled me for more than seventy years.

I was on my own.

As I had been for as long as I could remember.

"Your past." Helagon whispered it in such a way that I could hear him even where I lay, so far below. "I will reveal it to you, if you just give me the stone."

I knew Helagon was evil. I knew that if I gave in and let him have the stone, he would do terrible things. Even so, I will not pretend I was not tempted. What greater offer could there have been be than to finally, *finally* understand who I was, and where I'd come from?

"If that's not enough, consider this. I can restore your friend William to his body and wake the Baron from his fateful sleep."

I felt a new surge of fury. It was hard enough to resist what Helagon was offering me. How could I deny William the chance to regain his body? How could I leave the Baron in a sleep that would lead to death?

Unexpectedly, Karl gave me what I needed. From where he sat he murmured:

"The fate of all rests in their hands,
The cost so high, it stills the voice.
Long-buried hope makes sharp demands;
A breathless world awaits their choice. "

"Shut up!" snarled Helagon. Then he unleashed a bolt of power that sent Karl sprawling. The librarian lay where he fell, groaning. But Helagon had acted too late. I recognized the words. They were from the prophecy William had read the night we'd awoken the toad.

The world was in our hands.

My hands, now. And it was my job to save it from this madman.

But what had the world done for me? Why should I care what happened to it?

As the question burned inside me, I thought of Granny Pinchbottom, and how the idea of Helagon gaining power had filled her with fear. I thought of the Baron, slowly dying in his own bed from the spell Helagon had cast. I thought of the squirrels and the bear who had come to our aid. I thought of the forest and how I loved it. And I thought of what Stanklo had told us about the Pit of Thogmoth. Were the answers to the questions that wrung my heart worth the destruction of Nilbog?

Tears filled my eyes. My strange life had made me

sharp and secretive and bitter. But I could not give the world over to this monster.

"Fauna," Helagon whispered. "Oh, Fauna, I can do so much for you. I could be like a father to you. I could—"

Father? I had no father!

"Shut up!" I screamed in rage.

"That's not very polite, Fauna."

"It's not polite to want to open the Pit of Thogmoth! Why do you want to do that?"

"I think you will understand, dear. It's funny. In truth, you and I want exactly the same thing."

"What's that?" I asked, startled once more.

"To go home."

Yes, I did want a home. More than anything. I could not have it, not with my strange condition. But what could Helagon mean about himself?

"I don't understand," I said. "How would opening the Pit of Thogmoth take you home?"

"Because it's where I came from!"

With that, he spread his arms wide. A blaze of light flashed up around him.

When it faded, the handsome man was gone. In his place stood a terrifying demon, seven feet tall at least, his skin red and scaly, his yellow eyes blazing.

"The Pit of Thogmoth is my home, and I have been shut out of it for over two hundred years by the treachery of a small band of humans and goblins. Help me open it, Fauna, and I will put the world at your feet. You will be garlanded with jewels. I know people have been cruel to you, child. Now they will crawl before you. I can do so much for you. Just give me the stone!"

"Shut up!" I cried, horrified that he would think I would want such a thing. "Shut up and leave me alone, and *go back to where you came from!*"

Solomon's Collar tingled fiercely around my neck.

The Black Stone of Borea flared hot against my belly.

I screamed in pain.

But from Helagon there was only silence.

Cautiously I glanced up.

The wizard was nowhere in sight.

The dome, too, had disappeared. The goblins had stopped fighting, the angry cries of the red-headband crew now no more than confused whimpers.

I saw Herky capering atop the stone nose. "Herky back!" he cried. "Herky back!"

Above the little goblin's head fluttered Sterngrim.

Bwoonhiwda rushed to my side. "You did it, Fauna!" she said as she helped me to my feet. "You sent Hewagon away!"

"Is he really gone?" I asked, baffled, dizzy, not understanding.

Karl sat up, groaning. His black hair stuck out in all directions, and his face was smeared with soot. "You must have had some kind of power over the stone," he said. "As soon as you told Helagon to go back to where he came from, he vanished! I don't know where he went, but he's definitely gone. You were brilliant, Fauna!"

I shook my head. "Not brilliant, just lucky. Luck and having the collar . . . and the right words. Thank you for reminding me of what was in that book."

"That's what librarians are for," he said with a smile.

I was feeling very good until I looked over and saw Spirit-William kneeling next to his body. The red glow was gone; it had vanished with Helagon. It didn't matter—the time limit had passed, and William couldn't get back in. His face was twisted in despair.

My stomach knotted. I had banished Helagon but failed my friend.

Karl, who couldn't see William, said, "How in the world did the Black Stone get into Bwoonhiwda's braid?"

"I think I can answer that," said the toad. "Though I would rather do so from my human form."

"You can talk again!" I cried.

"Yes, Helagon's 'Speech be gone' spell vanished

when he was banished, if you will forgive the rhyme. The 'Speech be thine' spell went too. However, it woke something in my mind that did not go away."

"Unfortunately, we can't turn you back," Karl said. "William is trapped outside his body and can't re-enter it, which means he can't look at you in the mirror.

"Are you certain of that?" asked a new voice.

Sophronia shimmered into sight.

"Hello, love," said Edrick. "Nice to see you!"

"What ah you doing heah?" demanded Bwoon-hiwda. "We needed you ten minutes ago, not now!"

"I know, and I was trying desperately to reach you. But Helagon had set up a block against me. Not that I could have done much good—he is far more powerful than I. Besides, you did splendidly on your own. Especially you, Fauna."

I shook my head. "Helagon may be gone, but William was locked out of his body for too long. He can't get back in. Which means we can't return Edrick to his human form. Wait! Can *you* get William back into his body, now that we have the Black Stone?"

Sophronia shook her head. "I am not strong enough to use the stone. If I took it into my hands, it would absorb my power and destroy me. Edrick could do it if he were human."

"But we can't make Edrick human without William! It's like some horrible circle. We need Edrick to get William back into his body. But without William in his body, we can't restore Edrick!"

I expected Sophronia to react to this with tears, since her husband was trapped as a giant toad. Instead she said gently, "For every spell there is a counterspell to overcome it. This is the law of magic. Yes, William has been too long out of his body for the Sleep Walk spell. But that does not mean all is lost. Can you think of anything that might be stronger? Anything that might connect spirit to body once again?"

I knew she was hinting at something I should understand but didn't. "Can't you tell me?" I pleaded.

Sophronia shook her head, making her long red hair brush over her shoulders. "I can give you hints, but I can't tell you. The magic doesn't work that way."

"Oooh! Oooh!" Igor cried. "What about blue goo? It fix Baron. It fix Herky. Fix William, too?"

Feeling a surge of hope, I took the stuff out of my coat pocket. It was covered with lint. Hoping that wouldn't affect it, I stretched it to reveal a clean section, then snapped off a piece. Then I knelt beside William's body and pulled open his mouth to tuck the glob of goo between his lips.

"How will we know if it's working?" said Spirit-William, who was floating beside me.

"You'll just have to try to get back in, I guess."

His face a mix of hope and terror, he attempted to reenter his body. As soon as he hit the flesh, his spirit form was flung back just as it had been the first time he tried. Kneeling beside me, he buried his face in his hands and began to weep.

My heart ached for him.

Sophronia leaned close and whispered, "Do you remember how William healed the goblin king?"

"Of course. He had a golden collar that Granny Pinchbottom had given him. He used it to join the king's head to his body so that . . ."

Sudden hope flooded my chest. I also had a collar that came from Granny Pinchbottom! But what good could it possibly do William while it was locked around my neck?

I could think of only one thing to try.

It was time to tell the truth.

I took the Black Stone to Bwoonhiwda and said, "Hold this, please."

Then I returned to William and knelt beside his body. His spirit hovered over me, inner self staring down with sad, desperate eyes at outer self.

Putting my hands to the back of my neck, I looked up at Spirit-William and said, "This collar was meant for you. I did not mean to take it, but when I tried it on, it locked itself around my neck. It was wonderful, and terrible. It let me talk to animals but would choke me if I tried to tell a lie. You saw that happen the night of your party. So you know I am telling you the truth when I say this collar was meant for you and I am sorry that I took it. I should have told you right away."

The collar tingled around my neck, then opened and fell into my hands.

"Fauna!" said Spirit-William.

"Shhhhh . . ."

Turning to Igor, I said, "Lift his head, please."

Igor knelt beside William. With surprising gentleness he used his large, hairy hands to raise William's head from the ground.

Tenderly I placed the collar over my friend's throat, then pulled the ends around to the back of his neck.

As I brought them together, I heard a click.

They had locked into place.

William's spirit vanished.

An instant later a smile curved his lips. His real lips.

Opening his eyes, he spit out the blue goo and whispered, "You did it, Fauna!"

Goblins believe there is a place for everything, and everything should be in its place. This applies to people, too. Adventures are all fine and good, as long as you end up where you belong.

—Stanklo the Scribbler

CHAPTER TWENTY-ONE

THE LADY OF THE CASTLE

Igor swept William into his arms and leaped to his feet. Pounding William on his back, he shouted joyfully, "William real again! William real!"

Herky scrambled down the Big Face. "Butterhead boy back in body!" he cried, running in circles and waving his arms.

Sterngrim fluttered to my shoulder. She made a hissing sound, and I realized she was trying to talk to me. Only, I couldn't understand her now that I no longer had the collar. It made me a little sad.

"She said thank you for bringing her back," William called, still being held aloft by Igor.

More hissing.

246

"She says Helagon sent her someplace strange with too much light, but when you banished him, she popped back here." Turning to Igor, he said, "Put me down, please. I'm very happy to be real, but it's entirely due to Fauna."

I ducked my head and blushed.

William came and took my hands. "Thank you," he said softly.

"All right, I need a little help," Karl said. "Where's Helagon?"

"Fauna sent him away," said Sophronia. "Well, it was the combination of Solomon's Collar and the Black Stone that did the job. But it wouldn't have happened if Fauna hadn't resisted him and ordered him to go back to where he came from. It's funny— in a way that's what he wanted all along. That wasn't his real face, by the way. If he was from the Pit, I can guarantee he was in disguise. His real face would have been horrifying."

"I understand that," Karl continued. "But I still don't see how the Black Stone ended up in Bwoon-hiwda's bwaid—*braid*!"

"I can answer at least *part* of that," said Edrick-the-Toad, "and provide a few other answers as well. However, at the risk of repeating myself, I would be grateful if you would first return me to my true form. I've been waiting for quite a while."

Sophronia smiled. "Of course, darling." Turning to Karl, she said, "My thanks to you for bringing the mirror and the book. I've been waiting more than seven decades to use them!"

She walked over to Edrick and gave him a kiss.

"A kiss?" I cried. "Is that all it takes? Like in a fairy tale?"

Sophronia laughed. "That was just to show Edrick I love him, no matter what shape he inhabits. Still, I do prefer his true form. William, come stand here, please."

As Sophronia positioned William in the exact spot that she wanted, Karl walked over to me and whispered, "Look."

I glanced in the direction he indicated and saw Igor and Bwoonhiwda standing side by side. As Karl and I watched, the big woman took Igor's hand. To my surprise, he snatched his hand back. Then he fell to the ground and wrapped his arms over his head.

"What's wong?" Bwoonhiwda cried.

"Igor too happy! Don't know what to do!"

"Stand up, you big wug!"

Igor scrambled to his feet.

"Aw wight. That's bettah," Bwoonhiwda said, slipping her hand into Igor's once more. "Now wet's watch Sophwonia."

"If you two are quite ready, I'd like to get on with this," said Sophronia. But she was smiling as she said it. "Fauna, would you come here and hold the mirror, please?"

When I was in place, she said, "William, can you see Edrick in the glass?"

He nodded.

"And I can see William," Edrick confirmed.

"Then both of you hold still."

She opened the book—it clearly went right to the page she wanted—placed her finger in the middle of a page, and began to chant. Her voice was beautiful, and something about the words made my scalp tingle. I felt magic rise around us. Suddenly William cried out. A ray of white light burst from his chest, struck the mirror, bounced off it, and hit Edrick.

Sophronia continued to chant.

Rather than disappear, the light clung to Edrick. It spread over his huge, toadly body like melting butter. As it did, he screamed in anguish, the cry so painful I was sure Sophronia would stop chanting. To my surprise she kept on, raising her voice to be heard above it.

Edrick continued to scream. But he was also shrinking. Soon his face was an odd mix of toad and human. Soon after that he was human, but twisted and ugly . . . the disguise he had used when he'd been trying to find the Black Stone. After that the light grew too bright and I had to turn my eyes away.

I heard a buzz, then a loud snap.

Edrick stopped screaming.

When I turned my eyes back, he was fully human. However, a jagged scar stretched down the center of his handsome face. I realized it was a smaller version of the crack in the mirror, which made me feel guilty, since I was the one who'd broken it.

Sophronia either didn't notice the scar or didn't care, which I guess is more likely. Even with the scar, Edrick was very handsome. She hurried to his side, and for a minute they were busy being all husband-and-wifely.

When the two of them were finally done kissing, Edrick said, "My deepest thanks to all of you. It has been longer than I had expected since I've been able to stand on my own two feet."

Karl looked like he was about to burst. "*Now* will you explain how the stone ended up in Bwoonhiwda's braid?" he asked Edrick.

"I said I could tell you *part* of it, which is simply this: As soon as Fauna and William brought me to life, I spit the wretched thing out. It was like a fire in my gut."

As he said this, I remembered the clunk of something hitting the floor at about the time he started to move. Suddenly it all came clear to me! "I know what happened!" I cried. "When you spit out the stone, it ended up on the floor in front of the fireplace. Karl, do you remember how Bwoonhiwda's head tipped to the side when she wove the cannonball that killed Werdolphus into her braid? She looked for something of equal weight to balance it. The magical stone was the right size, and she chose it thinking it was just another cannonball."

"Hah!" exclaimed Werdolphus. "Good thing I offered to help! Otherwise you'd still be without the stone."

Bwoonhiwda stamped her foot. "But what now? The Bwack Stone wemains a tewwible thweat."

"Only if it stays in this world," Edrick replied. "Sophronia and I plan to take it elsewhere. It will be better for everyone that way."

"Elsewhere?" I asked.

Sophronia shrugged. "There are places magic-users

can go that most folks can't. Edrick and I will grieve to leave this green and lovely world behind. Even so, it will be better for everyone if the stone is gone. We long ago swore to do this if we ever succeeded in gaining the thing. We selected our place of retreat way back then. It's a small world but a pleasant one." She turned to Edrick. "Ready, darling?"

"Not yet, love. There's one more piece of information I need to pass along. Fauna, would you come here, please?"

I went to stand in front of him, wondering what he had in mind.

His next words made my knees go weak.

"I can tell you what Helagon would not."

I began to tremble. Was it possible that after all this time I would find out who I was and why I didn't age?

"Please," I whispered.

"You may not like what you hear. It was your own curiosity that got you into this."

"I still need to know . . . and to know if there is any way to change it."

"It's changed already."

"What do you mean?"

"I'll explain in a moment. Start with this: You were with me the moment I became the toad. You shouldn't

have been, but you sneaked into the tower where I was posing as the evil wizard. You came onto the roof at the very moment I threw the magic that Harry's mirror was designed to blast back at me. I was horrified to see you, but my shout for you to leave was cut off by my transformation."

As Edrick spoke, it was as if he was unlocking the doors of my memory. The moment came flooding back to me.

I remembered the light striking Edrick.

I remembered his cries of pain as his body twisted and turned into that of a giant toad.

And I remembered one more thing: who I really was.

I almost wished I hadn't. It was too strange. And what would the others think when they heard?

Edrick continued talking. "My theory—and it is only a theory—is that because you were right there when the Black Stone worked such powerful magic, that you were caught in the wave of that power. Then, when the stone was sealed inside my stony body, the magic that had caught you in its force was sealed as well, and it froze you as you were at that moment. When you and William released me and I spit out the stone, it released you as well. I suspect from that moment you began aging as normal."

Sophronia was looking at me in shock. "Edrick, you don't mean she's . . . ?"

"Yes, love. It's her."

Sophronia stared at me, then cried, "You're right! I couldn't see her at all when we were in Nilbog, and in this dim light—not to mention all the dirt on her face—I didn't see it! Gertrude! Thank the stars and powers we've found you!"

"Gertrude?" William said. "Who's Gertrude? Wait. Where did I just hear that name?"

"I believe that is for Fauna to tell you," Edrick said. "I can see by her face that she has remembered."

Everyone turned and stared at me. In the low light that came from the mushroom forest and the cliffside fungus, I could see the curiosity on their faces.

I took a deep breath. "Yes, I'm Gertrude. I'm the Baron's big sister."

Everyone burst out talking.

"Quiet!" roared Bwoonhiwda. "Wet Fauna speak!"

"I'm the Baron's big sister," I repeated.

"But how can that be?" William asked.

I turned to Edrick and Sophronia. "Can you help? It's still jumbled in my head."

"Of course, dear," Sophronia said. "At the time we were working out our plan to obtain the Black Stone, we felt it would be best to have a safe place to, um . . . *store* Edrick once he became a stone toad. Since we were good friends with the Baron's father, we asked if he would be willing to keep Edrick safe. The current Baron was little more than a baby at the time."

"We called him Bertie," I put in. "He was only about a year old."

Sophronia nodded. "He was a cute little fellow. Anyway, when we told the Baron's father our plan, he wanted to observe the magic in action. You wanted to come along too."

"Can you blame me?" I said. "It sounded fascinating."

"So what did you do?" William asked.

I winced at the memory. "When Father told me no, I hid in his wagon and secretly rode to Harry's village anyway. Father planned to position himself on a hill overlooking the town so he could watch what happened, but during the ride I decided to get even closer. So I slipped out of the wagon and made my way through the woods to the tower."

"Girl brave," Herky said.

"More foolish than brave. Truly, I didn't think it was that scary. Sure, everyone in the village believed there was a wicked wizard in the tower. But I knew it was just Uncle Edrick in disguise. And I knew he would never hurt me."

I was surprised when I heard myself call him "Uncle" Edrick. Until that moment I had forgotten that that was how I used to think of him.

"You were right, dear. I wouldn't have hurt you for anything. But that didn't mean I could protect you, with all that magic flying around!"

"I understand that now. It wasn't your fault."

"So what happened next?" William demanded.

"When the magic bounced back from the mirror and hit Edrick, I was caught in the backwash. It was as if my mind had been wiped clear. I didn't know who I was or why I was there. Terrified, I ran out of the tower and into the woods."

"And you've lived on your own ever since?" asked Sophronia in horror.

"Not entirely. A few times people took me in. But when they realized I was not getting any older, they would think I was some sort of witch child. I barely escaped with my life from the second home I stayed in. After that I did live on my own. It was safer."

"Well, you don't have to live on your own anymore," William said. "I'm sure the Baron will take you in."

Edrick and Sophronia laughed.

"What's so funny?" I demanded.

"It's Fauna who will have to take in the Baron," Edrick said to William. "As the elder child, she's the true owner of Toad-in-a-Cage Castle!"

"Baron not going to like that!" said Igor.

I didn't like it either. The idea made my knees weak. Then another thought hit me, a frightening one. "What if we can't bring the Baron out of that magical sleep?"

"I am certain he woke the moment you sent Helagon away," Edrick said. "Just as all the other spells ended at that time."

"He has always known it was a possibility his sister would show up," Sophronia added. "Though he assumed if she ever did, it would be as a woman almost ten years older than him, not as a child!"

"But what am I going to do with a castle?" I wailed.

"We'll help you," Karl said gently. Then he added, "I've seen your father's will. In fact, the Baron and I have discussed it many times. There won't be any question about it when we go back."

Bwoonhiwda pounded the butt of her spear against the ground. "You ah now the Wady of the Cassew!"

It took me a moment to realize she had called me "the Lady of the Castle."

I figured it might take another seventy-some years to get used to the idea.

"And now," said Sophronia, "it's time for us to leave."

She held out her arms. I ran to her and hugged her, the way I used to so long ago. Uncle Edrick bent and kissed me on the head. "Be good," he said, giving my hair a gentle tug.

Back when I was Gertrude, it had always made me laugh when he did that. Now it made me sad. "Do you really have to go?"

Sophronia had tears in her eyes. "I wish we didn't, dear. But this is the vow we made when we joined the League of Teldrum."

"Will you ever come back?"

Edrick shook his head. "That would raise the risk of another evil wizard finding the stone and coming after it. No, once there, we'll need to stay."

William took my arm. "Come on," he said softly, leading me back to the others.

Standing face-to-face, arms around each other, Sophronia and Edrick began to chant. As their voices blended, a swirl of white light rose around them.

A strange aroma, wild and spicy, filled the air.

An instant later they were gone.

After a long silence William said, "Well, Gertrude. That was interesting."

I smacked him on the arm. "The name is Fauna, and don't you forget it!" With a smile I added, "You big wug!"

So that's the story of how I became the Lady of Toad-in-a-Cage Castle.

When we arrived back at the castle a few days later—having been sure to return Flegmire's bucket—we were relieved to find that the Baron had made a complete recovery. I was afraid that when he learned I was his sister, he would faint again, but he actually seemed happy about it.

"I only wish Father were here," he said. "He never stopped hoping for your return, you know."

Hulda was delighted to have another female in the castle. As it worked out, she got two, since after Bwoonhiwda went to the queen to report on her mission, she returned to us. She is now in charge of castle defense. I don't really think we need much defending, but it's good to have her here. It certainly makes Igor happy.

Karl and William helped me write all this down. It has taken us a few months, and in that time I have grown about half an inch. It is very strange to be getting taller again after all these years.

Herky still lives with us and is as much of a menace as ever. And Werdolphus continues to haunt the castle. He says he'll move on when he's good and ready. Sterngrim, however, returned to the other lindlings. She told William she would miss us but didn't think it was possible for her to live aboveground.

As for me . . . well, it is strange to be living in the castle again. It is as if I am beginning my life all over. Mostly I like it. But sometimes I get restless and sneak away to spend a night or two in the forest.

I need to be alone to think.

What I mostly think about is this: I have been angry with the world for a long time.

Maybe it's time to stop.

A NOTE FROM THE AUTHOR

Goblins in the Castle, the first book about the strange doings in and around Toad-in-a-Cage castle, was published in 1992. Why return to that world now, more than twenty years later? Well, the truth is, Nilbog has never been far from my mind, and this is actually something I have wanted to do ever since the first book came out.

It was just that life, and other stories, always seemed to get in the way.

Well, that and the fact that I didn't know what happened next. All I knew was that whatever the plot turned out to be, it had to include Bwoonhiwda, who appeared one night when my wife and I were bouncing Nilboggian ideas around and making each other laugh hysterically.

Of course, having Igor living in the cellar beneath the cellar beneath the cellar beneath my house meant that I shouldn't have worried about it. Once again the time came when late one night he trundled up the stairs and plopped *Goblins on the Prowl* onto my desk.

I was astonished to find that this time Fauna had written the story . . . and even more amazed to discover her secret. (Really, I had had no idea!) But what delighted me most was finding the "story beneath the story" of the giant Harry. This was because my very first published book, *The Foolish Giant* (a picture book illustrated by my wife, Katherine), told the version of Harry's story that Bonecracker John relates in this book. What a shock it was to find the real version of Harry's story!

As is the way with books, this one still needed fine tuning and editing to make it worthy to see print, so I would like to acknowledge those who helped along the way.

First of all, there is my reading partner, Tamora Pierce. Tammy lives across the street from my office, and most weekdays when we are both in town we get together in the early evening to read our works-in-progress to each other. When Tammy groans at my jokes, or curses me for my cliffhanger chapter endings, I know I'm on the right track.

Then a very special thank-you goes to teacher Doug Hinton, who has been reading *Goblins in the Castle* to his classes every year for nearly two decades now. At this point Doug probably knows the text of the first book better than I do, and his input on this book was incredibly valuable. If Doug wasn't satisfied with what I had, then I knew it wasn't right yet . . . and when he was satisfied, I was very, very happy indeed.

And of course there is the editorial team . . . first Karen Nagel, who demanded I make it better, then the wonderful Amy Cloud, who told me when I had managed to do so.

Additionally, I have the great good fortune to be in two wonderful writers' groups, MFL and TOG. I received tremendous support and important input from both. Alas, I cannot reveal the meaning of "MFL" and "TOG" as those are deep, dark secrets. However, I can list the membership for each group. In MFL we have Cynthia DeFelice, MJ Auch, Vivian Vande Velde, Patience Brewster, Robin Pulver, Ellen Stoll Walsh, and Katherine Coville. The TOG team consists of Ellen Yeomans, MJ Auch, Amber Lough, Suzanne Bloom, and Laurie Halse Anderson. If you think I am lucky to be part of these amazing groups, all I can say is, "You're right!"

Last, but far from least, is my wife, author and artist Katherine Coville, who has been putting up with Igor's antics for over forty years now.

How could I do it without her?